# Blackout

I0742582

---

Hope A.C. Bentley

This is a work of fiction. All of the characters, organizations and events portrayed in this novel are either products of the author's imagination or are used fictitiously.

Published by
Golden Light Factory
East Burke, Vermont
www.goldenlightfactory.com

ISBN 978-1-7327645-4-5

To Dad, who keeps us going.

&

Rusty, Ted, Tyler and their families.
We're meeting in Vermont

# Chapter One: The Last Snickers

**Margot**

Everyone always asks where you were when it started.

I was sitting on the couch flipping through my mom's *Vogue*. I was looking at each page and deciding what I would want in my closet if I were a New York City socialite. It's a game my friend Judy and I used to play a lot together. We'd point at a skirt that cost $1,500 and try to imagine that a skirt could cost as much as Judy's brother's car. A watch can cost as much as a house. You can buy an ounce of skin cream or a week of groceries. Of course we made fun of people who actually bought the stuff, but still I was curious. What would it be like to look at something and not decide if you could afford it or even needed it? You could just look at the world and decide if you *wanted* it or not. I was pondering a pair of silver knee-high boots (a cool $950) when the phone rang.

I plodded over and checked the caller ID. It was my grandmother.

"Hey, Grandma," I said.

"Margot, are your parents home?"

I frowned. For one, Grandma usually called me Sweet Pea. Plus, she liked to chat, and I was pretty sure she liked me better than she liked Mom.

"No, just me." I paused, and it felt funny, but I asked politely, "Do you want me to take a message?

5

"No. No." There was another pause and I heard Grandma inhale. "Listen, Sweet Pea, have you been listening to the news?"

"No." Grandma didn't usually ask stupid questions.

"Well, listen, something bad is happening. Big blackouts. Maybe an attack of some kind but nobody knows who's doing it."

"Blackouts, like no electricity?" I asked.

"Yes, but everywhere. We probably have about an hour left of power. That's what they say on the news. I don't know about phones. So you listen to me. I've got to get some things together and then I'm coming up to you. You hear? I'm coming up and I'll hopefully be there tomorrow, maybe late. Tell your mother, okay?"

"Okay," I said. What else could I say? I knew my mom would be mad that her mom was coming up on short notice. Plus, Grandma was just up here a month ago, and Mom figured that that should let her off the hook for the rest of the summer.

"Okay, now listen."

"I'm listening, Grandma." That must have been the fourth time that she'd told me to listen.

"Margot, you get in the car. Take your brother—"

"He's at the Lawsons."

"Okay, get in the car and go get your brother. Do you have a credit card?"

"Yes," I said, a little nervous. "But I'm not supposed to drive without someone who has had their license—"

"It's okay, Sweet Pea, just do as I say. Go to the grocery store and get canned goods. Okay? Dried beans, canned fruit, rice, nonperishables." I could tell Grandma was thinking aloud. "Get salt, too, and soap. Dish soap, laundry detergent, get toilet paper, but get food first. Canned food that won't go bad."

6

"Grandma," I asked, "are you okay?"

"No, Sweet Pea, I'm scared. But you do as I say."

"I will. I will," I repeated.

"Get as much food as you can. I want you each to push two carts. Then you go to the pharmacy and you get first-aid stuff, you know what I mean?"

"Yes."

"Good. Then go to a gas station and fill up the car. And fill up a few of those portable gas cans. Then go right home. You got it?"

"Yes, Grandma."

Grandma sighed loudly. "Good girl," she said. "Now go."

The minute I hung up the phone, I got smacked by a wave of nerves. I'd never driven alone before, never grocery shopped before, never even gotten gas by myself.

I found the keys to my mom's minivan and then my wallet. I felt rushed, but for some reason I ran upstairs and put on a nicer shirt and some of Mom's lipstick. Don't ask, but it made me feel calmer.

I grabbed a bunch of grocery bags and then ran out to the car. I guess I thought the car would know that I wasn't supposed to drive, because when it started up without a problem, I was surprised. Driving alone for the first time made everything seem unfamiliar. Where was the Lawsons' house? Would I get arrested? Glancing nervously in the rearview mirror, I stopped at the stop sign at the bottom of our hill and wondered. Left or right? It wasn't a hard question, just one I'd never had to answer before.

I got to the Lawsons' without even passing another car, put the car in park, and let out a huge breath. I honked. Or I tried to honk, but I really just hit the horn a glancing blow. I pushed down hard and a blast came out that made me jump. My brother

7

and his friend came running around from the back of the house. Lucas stopped short when he saw I was driving.

"What are you—"

"Come on," I said. "Thank Mrs. Lawson and get in."

"Where's Mom?" asked Lucas suspiciously. He came closer and waved absently at Mrs. Lawson, who'd come out to the porch.

"I'll tell you in a minute, just get in."

Lucas scowled and didn't budge.

"Come on," I said. "You can ride in the front."

Lucas ran to the passenger door and hauled it open. He sat down and grinned at me for a second.

"Seat belt."

"Where's Mom?" asked Lucas, but this time without suspicion.

"She's playing tennis."

"You're not allowed to drive, you know."

"I know, but we have to go to town. Something bad is happening."

I told Lucas as best I could what Grandma had told me. He interrupted only once to ask, "You have a credit card?" and then he said that we should get beef jerky, too.


It turned out to be impossible to push two carts each, so after Lucas ran over my heel for the third time in one aisle, we gave up and each filled two carts one at a time. Most people looked like they were just doing their regular shopping, which made me feel even more conspicuous, dumping armloads of canned beans and giant bags of rice into a cart. The funny thing is that buying so much stuff makes you feel kind of powerful, so by the time we had filled up two carts, I was actually having fun. I grabbed some olive oil, because it seemed right, and some beef jerky to make Lucas happy. I got salt, and I would've gotten spices, but they were really expensive for just a little jar. I got coffee and tea, recognizing Mom and Dad's brands, canned fruit and vegetables, two of every kind of pasta, and every kind of sauce.

"Are you allowed to buy *vodka* spaghetti sauce?" asked Lucas.

I glared at him but put it back.

In the checkout the lady raised her eyebrows at our four carts but didn't ask me anything. She just talked over my head to another checker about the blackouts that were rolling up the coast.

"Texas? No electricity. Florida? Nothing. My sister's in North Carolina, and she just texted to say that the Internet is out too."

Lucas and I helped bag the groceries, and as we did, I noticed that people seemed to be streaming into the store in a hurry. The checker noticed too.

"Looks like you beat the crowd," she said cheerfully.

It turns out no one will stop you from doing something if you just act like it's normal, as if you drive without a license and spend hundreds of dollars on a credit card all the time.

At the pharmacy we sailed grandly around with our cart, picking out Band-Aids with superheroes, gauze, iodine, athletic tape, anything that seemed useful. Lucas and I gave the condom aisle a wide berth and grinned at each other a little. I got some cold medicine and some vitamins and was browsing through the pain relief aisle when all the lights in the store went out. My heart gave a little hiccup, and Lucas and I froze for a second.

A generator coughed to life somewhere and some dim lights came on along the walls of the store. Lucas and I hurried up to the front to pay. I hadn't really noticed, but by now the store was pretty crowded. We waited, and every second I got a little more nervous. I noticed that there seemed to be a lot of people gathering outside the liquor store next door. Every time somebody opened the door to the pharmacy, the sound of the crowd came in. Lucas and I stood our ground nervously until it was our turn.

"Do you have a savings card?" The checkout girl was plainly distracted and kept looking around us to see what was happening outside.

"No," I said politely.

We paid for everything with the credit card, and again, no problem from the checkout girl. It went so well that Lucas added two Snickers bars for us, and I just smiled at him. The whole time I was praying that Grandma was right and that there really was a huge emergency.

The last stop was gas. When I slowed down to turn into the station, I saw a guy waving everybody over to a line.

"'Lectricity's out," he called. "We just got the one pump on a generator."

This was bad news. It meant I was going to have to back the car up to the pump, which was never going to happen. Whenever I tried to go in reverse, everything just went, well, backward. I was debating whether or not to ask the guy if he could back up for me when I saw my softball coach two cars ahead of me in line. She was talking on the phone, looking the other way, but I knew if she saw me, she'd probably come over, and she'd know I wasn't supposed to drive. While I was trying to figure out if I should pull up into the line or just drive off, the guy behind me beeped really loud. I jumped about a foot and I saw Coach look up. I admit, I kind of panicked and I peeled out into the road without looking to see if it was clear. That meant another person honked at me.

We made it home with no more honking, but Lucas gave me a real *look* when we got out.

I poked my head inside the house and listened. I could hear someone in the shower upstairs, probably Dad.

"Lucas, help me put this stuff in the basement." For some reason I was whispering. Without talking, Lucas and I unloaded the gazillion bags into the basement and hid it all beneath a tarp. If the whole blackout didn't turn out to be an emergency, I needed time before I got caught for using the credit card. When we came inside again, Dad was prowling through the fridge.

"Power's out," he said casually, putting some sandwich stuff on the counter. I realized that our generator was on.

"Dad." I stared at him, and he stopped spreading mayonnaise on a piece of bread.

"What's up, honey?"

"Dad!" said Lucas, bouncing on his toes with excitement. "Something bad's going on, and Grandma's coming up, and Margot drove the car without you!"

"Lucas!" I shouted.

"Lucas, slow down," said Dad. A big glop of mayonnaise landed on the counter. "Margot, what—"

The telephone rang, and Dad shook his bread knife at me. "This is not over, young lady." He answered the phone and grimaced.

"Hello, Jeremiah." It was my uncle, Jerry. Uncle Jerry had once called my dad a Harvard-ass sissy—to his face. My dad calls Uncle Jerry a willfully ignorant redneck who reliably votes against his own best interests—but never to his face.

"Karen's not here. Can I—what? You're what? What in the hell is going on?" My dad sputtered at the phone and then looked at it in his hand. "Hello? Hello?"

11

Dad pinned me with a glare, and I was about to confess everything when I was saved again, this time by my mom.

She breezed in the door and propped her tennis racket against the wall. "God." She puffed air out of her mouth and rolled her eyes. "Everyone's all worked up about this *blackout* thing. Nancy was in such a tizzy to get home that I just said I would *walk* home, since we didn't get any *exercise* anyway."

Mom had been in an evenly matched battle against her weight for as long as I could remember. She wasn't fat exactly, but she had that kind of pregnant bump in front. She spotted my father and the mayonnaise. "I don't know why you go mountain biking and then come home and eat mayonnaise. It's fat, *pure* fat."

"I bike *so* that I can come home and enjoy . . ." My dad started to say what he always said when my mom attacked him about his sandwiches, but stopped. "Karen, Jeremiah just called. He's on his way out here. Lucas says that your mother called—"

"I talked to her," I interrupted. "She's getting some things together and coming up tomorrow."

Mom frowned "Here? I wish she'd asked. When?"

"Karen, what are these blackouts about? We need to talk to Leah," said Dad. I could tell that the worry was starting to reach him, even if it had glossed right over Mom.

Mom waved her hand at him. "Oh, I did. *Everyone* was calling *everyone* at the tennis courts, so I called Leah. The school line was busy, but I called her phone and she said not to worry. They're shutting down the school, of course, but . . ." Mom paused dramatically. "She's going to be picked up in a *helicopter* by the *senator!*" Mom smiled triumphantly.

Sometimes I wished my mom would listen to herself speak. I wondered if she would notice that she was living in a fairy tale where my sister was concerned.

12

Leah was currently staying in Maine at a "minimum-security prison for the rich and deranged" (her words) or a "year-round therapeutic boarding school" (Mom's words).

"The senator?" said Dad with a cough.

"Senator Davenport. Remember? He's from New Hampshire? A Republican? His son is apparently a good friend of Leah's."

"Senator Davenport?" Dad started to run his finger down the  phone list taped by the kitchen phone. "I would be delighted . . ."—he paused to dial—"delighted but very, very surprised if she were, in fact, being whisked away by 'the senator!'" Dad sucked in a breath and frowned at the phone. "The phone is dead! Karen, what did she say exactly?"

Mom and Dad planted their feet at each other and squared off for an argument. I took Lucas by the shoulder and steered him out to the back porch.

"We should turn the generator off, maybe," he said. "Save gas."

I shrugged. Lucas walked over to the generator and fiddled with it for a minute. The generator coughed and was quiet. Lucas can be pretty smart for a ten-year-old sometimes.

We ate our Snickers bars in the silence, looking out over the valley below.

# Chapter Two: 2,384 Miles

### Caleb

Let me tell you about all the layers of bored there are in my dad's house.

For one, there is this stupid Nintendo game from the nineties or something that my dad unearthed for us to play together. Super Mario Bros. The pixels are so huge that I can see them even on my dad's eighteen-inch TV. That is the first layer of bored.

Then there is this room, where I have been for about forty-eight hours. It's "my room," but it's also the living room and most of the kitchen and also it has the door to the outside, so really, it is not my room at all, just a spot for me to *not* sleep on the pullout couch that feels like a lumpy canoe.

Then there is this house. It smells like motor oil because it also happens to be my dad's business. The house is the upstairs. The garage is the downstairs. There's no yard, just a big, baking-hot parking lot.

If that's not enough boredom for you, take a look at the town of Alameda. Besides my dad's shop there is a gas station, which is also sort of the grocery store and which rents out actual VHS videos. It's also the liquor store and coffee shop. There are about twenty houses, three of which are hair salons.

Then there is the whole state of Wyoming, which as far as I can see is flat, dry, and windy. And hot. And boring.

I have twelve more days of this before I can go back to Park City with my mom. I have to visit my dad three times a year, starting from when they got divorced five years ago, when I was six. It has gotten worse every year.

I get up and pick up a magazine off the floor. It's *Sports Illustrated*, but it is almost nine months old. I look out the window at the front of the house. A squirrel runs across the street. I look down into the parking lot below. No Dad, but I can hear clanking noises, which means he's working on something in the garage.

The phone rings. It's super loud so that Dad can hear it when he's under a truck or something. I jump about a foot in the air and drop the magazine. After a million rings I hear Dad answer on the garage line. I pick up the magazine and toss it onto the coffee table in front of the TV. It slides off onto the dirty carpet. I flop onto the bed and bang my elbow on something hard in the mattress. Again. I can hear my dad coming up the steps outside, so I sit up and try to look interested in something.

"That was your grandma out in Connecticut." Dad stands in the door, rubs some grease on the rear of his jeans, and adjusts his baseball hat. He looks confused for a minute and then crosses over to the TV and flicks it on. A tiny spark flashes in the middle of the screen and then grows slowly into a dim picture. This is normal.

"Your grandma said something about blackouts all over the States. Said we should pack up the truck and head out to Vermont."

The picture on the screen materializes into a nicely dressed man with a microphone. Behind him is a huge room of people who are so packed together that you could probably crawl across the top them.

"As you can see behind me, Grand Central Station is completely packed with people trying to get off the island in response to the news of massive blackouts that are sweeping the nation."

The screen cuts to a shot of cars all lined up and not moving on a bridge.

"Officials have directed all but one lane of the George Washington Bridge to accommodate outgoing traffic. They warn that cell coverage could go down at any moment, so they are advising that families designate—"

Abruptly the screen fills with black-and-white fuzz.

I look at my dad.

He takes off his hat and says, "Huh."

"What did Grandma say about Vermont?"

Dad walks over to the fridge and takes out two cans of beer. He tosses me one without thinking and opens the second. I catch the can with one hand, but I don't think my dad notices. I put it down on the coffee table.

"She said to buy a bunch of gas, get in whatever wreck I've got that will make it to Vermont, and meet everybody at Karen's house."

I have to admit I get a little bit excited about getting out of Alameda, and I can tell Dad is actually considering it. I'm just about to ask if we'd still be back in twelve days to see Mom when the phone rings again. Dad picks it up.

"'Lo?" he says.

I can hear my mom's voice all the way across the room. I can tell she's upset, but I can't hear what she's saying.

"Yeah, he's right here. He's fine." Dad looks at me. "I got him, Alice. We're fine out here. Nope, no riots and plenty of food. My mom wants us to go to Vermont, to Karen's place." Dad turns and looks at me. I can see a deep wrinkle between his eyebrows. "Yeah . . . well, you know my mom, but if this whole thing seems serious, we could meet you out there. It's Canton Hollow, Vermont." Then Dad says louder, "CANTON HOLLOW . . . CANTON . . ." Then Dad looks at the phone and I know that he's lost the connection.

I run over, grab the phone, and dial Mom's cell. It just rings and rings.

Once I got lost at a county fair when Mom and Dad were still together. One minute I was following Dad's legs through a crowd, the next minute I couldn't see much except a pen of sheep. I waited for the legs to clear out of the way, and when they did, I couldn't see Mom or Dad anywhere.

I was scared then, but I'm terrified now.

"What happened to Mom?" I am still holding the phone, not looking at my dad.

"I think she was somewhere real crowded and folks started to panic." I am always surprised at how my dad just tells me the truth instead of changing his words to make them less scary for me, like Mom would. I'm glad about that now.

"Is she going to be all right?"

"I don't know, bub, but she is smart and tough and I wouldn't bet against her in any fight."

My shoulders start to shake a little.

"She'll be fine. We'll be fine."

Dad drains the beer that I left on the coffee table and stands up. He looks outside, frowning. "I guess I just told your mom we're going to Vermont." Dad slaps his hat back on his head and says, "We'll take the bike. Get packed."

# Chapter Three: Mistake #874

### Leah

"Yeah, Mom, I'll be fine. I'll call when I know which airport." Leah ended the call and tossed her phone onto Regan's bed.

Regan snorted. "It's a good thing that she doesn't actually know the senator's son. That kid's a freak."

"Trust me, she stopped listening when she heard the words 'private helicopter.'"

"You're nuts, Leah. I can't believe that you would rather stay here, by yourself, at dear old Wiltmore than go home."

Leah groaned. "I know. Maybe it's stupid, but can you believe—there are massive blackouts spreading across the nation, and my mom says that she can't cancel her tennis game and come get me? 'Nancy sooo depends on these little romps for her blood pressure,' she says. And oh, she'll have to cancel with *Linda*, but *maybe* she and my father could figure out a way to pick me up *somehow*." Leah stood up and snatched a bottle of nail polish of the dresser. "She literally drives me crazy. She'll never let me forget what a huge inconvenience I am to her."

"So you told her you're getting a ride home in a helicopter with a New Hampshire senator?"

Leah laughed guiltily. "Yeah. You don't happen to have a private jet or anything do you?"

Regan stuck out her tongue. "I wish. Just a humble old Town Car for me." Regan finished painting her nails a shiny black and began waving them gently over the desk. "But seriously, what are you going to do?"

Leah tossed the bottle of nail polish onto Regan's dresser and flopped back onto the bed. "I don't know. I'm sort of surprised that she actually believed me. My dad's pretty smart. He'll probably come get me soon. And in the meantime maybe I'll make Mr. Tanden fall madly in love with me." Leah struck a pose on the bed and Regan laughed.

"Daddy's not a senator, but you could probably come home with me. You might catch an eating disorder, though."

"Not funny, Regan."

"No, you won't catch it from me. I'm cured, remember? It's my mom you've got to worry about."

"I'm good staying here. Thanks, though."

Regan stood up from her desk and studied her hands. "Do me a favor?"

"What?"

"Can you zip my bag for me? I don't want to wreck my nails. My mom thinks black nail polish means I'm a lesbian devil worshipper."

Leah zipped Regan's enormous duffel bag and slung it over her own shoulder. They walked down to the main hall of the dorm and checked out with Ms. Goss, the dorm head.

"Oh good. You two are the last ones. Don't forget to pick up your meds from the infirmary. They must be surrendered to a parent or guardian, so don't get any ideas." Ms. Goss scrabbled a pile of papers together and hurried back into her apartment. She was probably leaving too, just like most of the other faculty and

19

staff. Leah waited until Ms. Goss had closed her door behind her, and then dropped Regan's duffel.

"I'll see you after the end of the world," she said.

Regan and Leah hugged.

"Good luck," called Regan as she hurried down the steps to the car waiting for her.

Leah waved and then turned and went back up the stairs to her own dorm room. The whole dorm was strangely quiet. It even smelled different without the other girls there.

Thanks to the fact that there really was a senator's kid at the school, Wiltmore had gotten a two-hour head start with the warning about the threat of blackouts and loss of communication all over the United States. There had been an all-school meeting that morning in which students had been informed that the school was closing and that they'd have to make plans to get home as soon as possible. The dorm heads had returned all cell phones to the students and then instructed them to pack, and check out before they left. Knowing that her cell phone was in her mother's name, Leah had simply called the dean of students and told him that Leah Deford would be picked up by her parents in a car. It would have been true if her mom hadn't irritated her so much. Leah didn't know why she had lied about the helicopter, but in fact, there had been two helicopters landing on the athletic field to whisk away certain students. Three vans had brought most of the students to the airport, and there had been a steady stream of cars picking up the students who lived nearby or could afford hired cars. Leah was neither.

Back in her room, Leah lay down on her bed and listened for any signs of life. She heard Ms. Goss drag a suitcase down the steps and then walk rapidly away to the faculty parking lot. Occasionally a shout and the sound of another car wafted in the window, then eventually nothing but birds.

She'd lied to her mother out of habit and maybe to see if her mom would really fall for the story. Now she wondered if she hadn't made a mistake. Leah sighed and rolled over. She picked up her phone and thumbed it to life. Should she call home? Was this a bigger mistake than she thought? Leah tossed her phone onto her desk. One more mistake on top of all the others would hardly make a difference. In minutes Leah was asleep.

She slept through the last hour of electricity, the last hour of phones, the last hour of Internet. When she woke up, it was almost dark, the lights didn't work, and she was totally alone.

# Chapter Four: No More Yogurt

### Margot

After checking to see if my parents were done arguing, I went inside to find some lunch. Dad was nowhere to be seen, his sandwich stuff abandoned on the counter. I opened the fridge and peered inside.

"Eat the yogurt, will you?" called Mom from the kitchen table.

I got out some yogurt and started to eat it, but the idea of it being a little warmer than it should have been was disgusting. I dumped it into the garbage and got some crackers instead. I watched Mom for a while as I munched a Triscuit.

Mom finished writing something on a list and then gave me a big *Guess what?!* face. I stared at her.

"I'm going to throw a Blackout Blowout Party!" Mom put her hands up like she was reading the name of the party off a marquee. I lifted an eyebrow to indicate my lack of enthusiasm. Mom clapped and gave a little laugh.

"We've got to eat all that stuff that is going to rot in the freezer, so I thought, why not have some folks over? What do you kids want to drink? I've got to find some cold beer and ice. What do you like? Punch? Juice?"

"What about those lemon and orange Italian sodas?" I said. There was about a five percent chance Mom would remember, because she was already sweeping her list off the table and packing her purse.

"Soda. Check. Well, I'll be back soon. I left a list for everybody." Mom fluffed out her hair and breezed out the door. Mom always acted like the star of her own reality television show.

I went around and checked everything again. None of the phones worked; my laptop wouldn't even turn on, and it smelled funny. No electricity since Lucas turned off the generator.

Dad came in, muttering about conservation measures. He's a professor of environmental science at the community college, and I think he was actually pretty excited about everybody going without electricity for a few days.

"Mom just went off to buy beer for a party," I told him.

"We've got to go get Leah. Is she filling up on gas?" he sputtered. He ran out to try to catch her, but I knew he wouldn't.

The door slammed and I heard my dad shouting. It's embarrassing, really, to have a dad who's such a pushover. I wished that for once he'd stand up to Mom, because Mom was the only one who believed that Leah was on her way home in the private helicopter of some senator. A sliver of worry worked its way in between my shoulders. It could be true, but what if it wasn't?

I closed up the box of crackers and looked around the kitchen. The natural thing to do at a time like this was to call Judy, my best friend. I checked my phone again, but nothing was working. Dad came back in and tried to call Leah three times in a row, but nothing was working for him, either. We were miserable together, sitting in the kitchen with our lifeless gadgets, when Lucas bounded in with a headlamp and a tool belt.

"Dad, can we get water without electricity?"

Dad looked at Lucas and frowned.

"Yes. Well—I'm not sure. We've got a well, I know, but it must use a pump, so—no, Lucas. I don't know."

"I'm going to go find a spring, then," said Lucas, and he ran out the door like the blackout was the best thing that ever happened to him. Dad went back to staring at the phone, but I could see Lucas's question buzzing around him like a mosquito. Sure enough, after thirty more seconds he threw down the phone and jumped up from the table.

"How the hell *do* we get water?" he muttered, and then he stomped off, shouting, "Where do we keep the manuals in this house?"

That got me thinking: Could we flush toilets without electricity? Take showers? I flipped open my dad's laptop before I remembered I couldn't Google anything with the Internet out. I tried to think about how people had learned things they needed to know before the Internet, and I realized Dad was probably right. We needed a manual. It seemed exhausting. I slumped at the table and felt the boredom start to smother me like a thick fog.

I looked in the fridge, staring blindly until I remembered that the power was off and closed the door with a guilty slam. I thought about the yogurt I'd thrown away, and all the food Mom wanted us to eat in one night. How did people store food in the olden days? Blocks of ice, maybe? That was no good.

Vaguely, I remembered my Laura Ingalls Wilder books, *Little House on the Prairie* and the others. I remembered that they smoked meat in a hollow tree. Since I couldn't think of anything better to do, I wandered to the bookshelf upstairs to see what I could learn.

It turned out that old Laura Ingalls Wilder gives a pretty good description of how to smoke meat in *Little House in the Big Woods*. You need salt and a hollow tree and a way to hang the meat inside the hollow tree, and then you need hickory chips, green ones that smoke a lot.

I kept reading, and before I knew it, I was halfway through the book and drenched in sweat because the sun had shifted around to pour right in my window. I didn't know if it was okay to take a shower or not, and the only sign of Dad was a note saying he'd gone to the small local airport to look for Leah. I had that really awful nervous BO from driving. The only thing for it was to ride my bike down to the small river that went through Canton Hollow and jump in.

At this point I should mention that I have huge boobs, and when I ride a bike, they hang straight down and bounce like two fleshy Slinkies. Trust me, they were not my idea. My boobs showed up overnight last January like a late Christmas present. But if they were presents, then they were the kind that your grandma picked out, three sizes too big for you to grow into. Anyway, I still hadn't figured out what to do about the Slinky effect, and sometimes on hot days they made me feel almost claustrophobic, like someone else was standing too close. In short, I could not wait to jump into the water.

I coasted most of the way down into the village and passed the gas station. A line of cars was parked there waiting to fill up. The gas pump was running on a propane generator, and a sign said, CASH ONLY, $4 A GALLON. There was a small group of people chatting by the pump. I coasted slowly by on my bike, wondering if I should get in line and buy gas. I had twelve dollars in my pocket. Would three gallons of gas be useful, providing I could find a container? I paused uncertainly in the shade of the gas tank canopy.

"Any ideas about the cause of this whole thing?" asked Mr. Fowler. He was an older guy who always drank coffee in the gas station for a few hours every morning.

"Well," said Tom, the owner of the gas station, "I don't think it could be terrorists. From what I know, it's too widespread and there are no direct attacks anyone's heard of."

Everyone nodded, but Mr. Fowler said, "Could just be starving us out, weakening us before they attack."

Tom shook his head. "Think of how sophisticated this has been. I heard on my CB radio that the whole United States lost electricity in a matter of hours."

"There's blackouts everywhere?" asked a woman.

"From what I know," said Tom gravely. "Actually, now that I think about it, they may have gotten satellites, too. They had to, to cut cell service."

"Naw, cell service is line of sight, like radio."

A few people nodded.

"Could be aliens," ventured another guy I didn't know.

"I think it's that rich idiot we supposedly elected," said the woman. "He's ruining the whole country."

I took that as my cue to go swimming.

A small, sunlit river ran behind the gas station, which was also a general store. The river was behind a row of trees, and just a little downstream was an old dam, which made a nice chest-deep swimming hole. I took off my shoes in the shade of the trees and hobbled over the rocks out to the deep part. I dove in without even waiting. I was that hot. The water was bracingly cold and the perfect cure for how sweaty and gross I'd been feeling.

I wished we could turn on the conditioning back home. We didn't usually need it in Vermont, but today it wouldn't be bad to have it on after I rode home up the hill. *What about the folks down south?* I wondered. I paddled against the current, trying to stay even with a log on shore.

Slowly the heat and sweat left my body. I ducked my head under the water one last time, savoring the quiet, then hobbled back over to my shoes. It was a long, slow ride back up the hill.

When I got to the house, the Murphys were there and Mom was in full Mom Show mode. She was running around telling everyone she'd had to drive to five different places to get cold beer and acting like this was a noble crusade.

I hadn't expected the Murphys. They had nothing in common with us and not really anything in common with each other. Mrs. Murphy was as thin and bent as a shepherd's crook and scurried everywhere she went like she was expecting to get stepped on by an enormous boot. Mr. Murphy was medium height with broad shoulders and the kind of jaw that you see in cologne commercials. He always seemed to take up more than his fair share of space in a room, and my mom had the world's most obvious crush on him. They had a kid Lucas's age and an older son named Ronan.

Ronan Murphy was a senior who was a big deal on the soccer team. He was medium height with really broad shoulders and his dad's jawline, but not his dad's beer gut. I always expected that someone who was so good looking would be a little more popular, but there was something serious about Ronan Murphy, like he was a man already and the rest of us in high school were just kids.

Anyway, Dad had worked with Mrs. Murphy on some local food or nutrition project, and then my mom had dug her claws in, and so that's how we knew them. Or sort of knew them. I waved to Mr. and Mrs. Murphy, who were out on the porch, and turned to run up to my room and change. My T-shirt

27

was wet and sticky, my face was sweaty from riding up the hill from town, and goodness knows what my hair was doing. So that was what I looked like when I opened up the front door of my house and saw Ronan Murphy in the flesh, staring forlornly at his phone in our mudroom.

If there is anything witty to say when you look like a drowned horse in front of the captain of your school's soccer team, I don't know what it is. I gawped at him, crossed my arms over my chest, and shuffled past him, hoping, praying, that his phone was working and that he was too distracted to notice my steaming, slightly fishy-smelling T-shirt.

I put some serious consideration into locking myself in my room and never coming out again, but I was starving and thirsty and irritated at my mom. Why in the world did she invite the Murphys? Why in the world didn't Ronan Murphy have anything better to do than to come to a lame Blackout Blowout Party?

I brushed the river detritus out of my hair and then tried on four different shirts before giving up. It's the boob thing. I can wear a regular old T-shirt and look like a well-upholstered armchair, or I can wear something more girly that makes people act like my boobs are aggressive animals that will attack if they maintain eye contact too long. I didn't have enough energy for that, so I went Armchair.

More than ever I wished Leah were home. Leah can do this thing where she wraps her wavy brown hair around her fingers a few times, twists it into a bun with an elastic, and voilà, she has the perfect hairdo. She can also talk to people without changing her personality like Mom does. Leah is always Leah. If she were here, she'd know how to be around Ronan Murphy without being distracted by his mysterious, sultry frown, which jangled my nerves like some sort of inner-ear problem.

I tried the twisty thing with my hair, which is thick and the color of dead grass. I ended up with a tangle the size of my fist, so I just tied that into place at the nape of my neck, heaved a sigh, and went downstairs.

The adults were all on the back porch, talking about the blackouts, of course. Sure enough, Mom had forgotten about the drinks I said I liked, and gotten us all juice boxes. I picked out a juice box and wandered into the front yard where Lucas and the Murphy kid were trying to play badminton. Feeling like I was six years old, I stuck the straw into the top of a box and slurped. Wouldn't you know, I was slouched over my stupid juice box when Ronan hopped lightly down the steps behind me.

He was even better looking up close. I noticed a little dimple, but just on one cheek, and some sweet crinkles at the corners of his eyes. His bottom lip stuck out more than his top one, wet and smooth, like a hard candy that had been licked. It drew my attention just hanging there, making me want to taste it.

"You want to play?" he asked, nudging one rippling shoulder toward the badminton.

I laughed like he'd just told a joke, then squinted at him through that hotness haze and realized he needed a yes or no answer.

"Oh, yeah, okay."

We batted the birdie around awhile, but I have never been able *not* to take a sport seriously. After my second diving save I finally I made a lame excuse and ran, literally ran, around the house to the back porch.

Mom had passed out drinks to everyone and had a few herself. There was still no sign of Dad or Leah.

"The bank was mobbed," I heard her say. "Luckily, the branch manager is a close friend of mine and I was able to get out a big wad of cash," she giggled stupidly, holding out her hands to show how big the wad of cash was and nudging Kevin Murphy.

I sighed. If Leah were here, she'd say something funny about it so that we could be a little less embarrassed. Watching your mother flirt is like seeing animals having sex. If they knew how dumb they looked, they probably wouldn't do it in public.

Thalia Murphy looked worried, but she barely seemed to notice my mother slavering over her husband. Suddenly I felt the electricity of Ronan, and sure enough, he was standing by my elbow. He must have seen me looking at his mom, because he glanced that way and frowned.

"She's worried because of me," he said. I almost did that thing where you look around to see who someone is talking to. Frankly, I wanted him to ignore me so I could get through the evening without further humiliation. Instead I just looked at him blankly.

"I have this medication I have to take every day, and my mom's worried we'll run out before they fix this." Ronan sighed and huffed a glossy lock of dark-blond hair out of his liquid brown eye.

"Oh," I said brilliantly. Was it polite to ask why people needed medication?

"So what do you think? Aliens? Al-Qaeda? Internet nerds?"

"You mean who did this? It's probably my sister, actually," I said, surprising myself with a joke.

Ronan quirked up the corner of his mouth, deepening his one dimple. "I guess that's one way to save the environment."

"Yeah," I mused. I had forgotten that Leah used to be really into the environment, before all the trouble and Janie. Ronan and I walked over to a part of the yard where we couldn't hear my mom being stupid.

"Juice box?" I offered.

He raised an eyebrow and actually smiled.

"Might be our last one of these for a while," he said, holding up his juice box for a toast.

I bonked my juice box against his and intoned, "To the last juice boxes in the world."

He put the straw right in the center of his bottom lip, and I tried not to stare at it.

Mom wobbled over with a plate of hamburgers, and Ronan and I both took one. Mine was so overcooked on one side it was like eating a hoof. I gave Ronan a nervous grin and went in search of the ketchup.

I'd just spotted the condiments when another car came down the driveway. Mom's tennis friend stepped out of her car and marched toward the porch. She was wearing a blue button-front shirt and khaki pants, which was totally out of character.

"Carol!" shrieked Mom. "Come join us!" Mom looked like someone who'd just been pulled over and had a body in her trunk and a burned-out headlight. She knew she was in trouble, since she hadn't invited her friend, but didn't know how much trouble.

"I'm here on official business," said Carol, smoothing down her front, then holding up a piece of paper. "I've been deputized to spread the word. These blackouts are serious." She cleared her throat and then read from the piece of paper.

"'Dear Citizens of the United States: As of today, our entire nation has lost power. Most communications have been compromised. You should expect to be without power for the foreseeable future and we urge you to take precautions. Signed, the Secretary of State.'"

At least Carol's outfit was explained. I understood then that it was her best approximation of a uniform. The rest of it defied understanding. The *entire* United States? No power for the foreseeable future?

There was a sticky silence like after somebody has been slapped on the cheek with a glove. Mom rose to the challenge.

"Carol, dear, join us for a bite. We're eating up the meat from the freezer."

"I can't stop. I'm notifying all of Canton Hollow tonight. There will be safe drinking water at the library within two days. Do you know how to dig a latrine?"

Mom laughed. "Of course!"

I suppressed a snort.

"Alright then, I've got to keep going." Carol might have made off with the moral high ground but she ruined it with a boast. "They offered me three gallons of gas to do this, but I volunteered."

"Well—great," Mom croaked.

The was another creaking silence before Carol performed a sort of boot-clicking turn and strode back to her car.

The porch erupted in talk. A half a cup of ketchup landed on my burger. Ronan appeared again.

"Whoa," he said.

I studied my burger. "Yeah. Crazy."

"My dad can't wait to go all GI Joe if this really is serious," said Ronan.

"Really? My dad can't even figure out how our well works." I took another bite of burger but gave up when my teeth hit solid charcoal. I put my plate on the porch railing.

"It's a good idea, though, to eat all this food, right?" Ronan popped the last bite of his burger into his mouth, and I watched him chew, enviously. "We've got a freezer of venison from last fall. We'll probably have to throw half of it away."

"Could you smoke it?" I asked, like I was an expert.

"Smoke it?"

"Yeah, you salt it, then hang it over a smoky fire for, like, a week. I was thinking of doing it for the rest of the meat in our freezer." I found that if I didn't look at Ronan's lips, I could make a complete sentence.

"Cool. We should totally do that."

The next thing I knew, I was tromping through the woods with Ronan Murphy, looking for a hollow tree and telling him everything I knew about smoking meat. Without meaning to, I invited him to bring over his meat. I actually said "You can bring your *meat*," for goodness' sake. Then just like that, we had plans for tomorrow. Lord, help me. It really was the end of the world.

# Chapter Five: Still 2,384 Miles

### Caleb

I wish I could undo all my thoughts about being bored. I'd take back every last think I thought about pixels and VHS and lumpy canoes and only think nice thoughts if it meant I could go back to being bored instead of terrified. I'm so worried about Mom that it feels like something's scraping at my chest with hot knives.

"Please, Dad," I beg again. "Please, we've got to go get her."

"Caleb, dammit, I said no!" Dad is stuffing some clothing into a brown paper bag. He crosses to the kitchen and cracks another beer. After a long swallow he looks at me and something breaks in his expression. "Listen, bub. I know you want to go get your mom. I do too. I mean, she was my wife, dammit. But I'm pretty sure that she can take good care of herself."

I start to cry. I can't help it.

"Now, listen. We don't even know where she is. She's traveling for work this week. Boston, she said?"

I wipe my nose and nod, looking at the ground.

"Do you know where she's staying?"

I shake my head. I never know where she's staying, just when she'll be home, which is supposed to be two days before Dad drives me back to Park City.

"So we don't know where she is. We don't know if the planes are going anywhere, but I'd guess not. She knows where we're going. I told her we're headed to your aunt Karen's place in Vermont. So I'm betting that the second she can, your mom will be on the first plane to Vermont. She might even get there before we do." Dad rubs the top of my head. I let him. "I guess that means we'd better listen to Grandma."

I scrub my face with my T-shirt and check the phone one last time. I pull my duffel out from beneath the pullout couch and stuff my clothes inside. Dad pulls out another beer and looks in the freezer.

Dad puts all the food in his kitchen, which isn't much, into a trash bag. I think at first that he's throwing it away, but then realize that that is my dad's style of packing.

"Can opener," I say.

"Glad I got you around," says Dad, grinning. He takes a box of bullets off the top of the fridge and starts a pile of stuff by the door. Paper bag of clothes, garbage bag of food, bullets.

"Power's out," he says. "Might as well eat this ice cream before we hit the road." He slaps a whole carton of rocky road ice cream down on the kitchen table and grabs two spoons. I try to eat some, but I can't. Dad throws down his spoon too.

"Doesn't feel right, does it?" he says.

"Nope."

"Well, let's get outta here."

We go down to the shop, and Dad rustles around in a big storage shed for a minute before he comes out with two sleeping bags and a gun and some other stuff I vaguely remember from a doomed camping trip we took last summer.

"Find as many of these as you can, will you?" He holds up a gas can.

I hunt around the shop and find six five-gallon gas cans, while Dad ties our stuff onto a little trailer. I realize all of a sudden that we are taking a motorcycle across the country. My throat closes with dread, but I feel a little excited, too. It seems too quick, because the next thing I know, my head is rattling around inside a motorcycle helmet and we're headed down Main Street pulling a little trailer. I hang on to my dad for dear life even though we're not going very fast yet.

Dad pulls into the gas station behind a line of two other cars. I didn't know that there were that many people in Alameda, but it seems like everyone wants gas. Dad hands me two twenties and tells me to get him a coffee, some food, and anything else I can't live without.

I go inside, and it seems like the whole town is in there yelling their opinions at one another. Everybody's got a different idea about what kind of gun you need to protect yourself from terrorists. The ammo behind the counter is flying off the shelves. I get some cans of stew, some chips, a bunch of candy bars, and Dad's coffee and then wait in line.

The store guy rings me up and then asks if I'm Jerry's kid. I say yes. He grabs a handful of tiny bottles of Canadian Mist whiskey from behind the counter and puts them in the bag too.

"Tell 'im those are from Earl," he says. "Good luck, little feller." He waves as I head out the door.

I give Dad the coffee and eat a Reese's peanut butter cup while he drinks coffee and fills up all our gas cans. When he is finished, he goes around the back of the gas station and takes a leak, then goes inside to pay for the gas. I don't know why, exactly, but I hide the whiskey in my backpack while he's gone. I hope Earl didn't see me. Having a secret makes me feel a little better when I climb on the back of the motorcycle and roar off down the road to Vermont.

# Chapter Six: Mistake #875

### Leah

Running her hands along the wall, Leah walked through the pitch-black hall of the dorm toward the red glow of the exit sign. She paused in the stairwell and listened. Nothing. Outside it was dusk and she could see well enough. It seemed as if every last person had left campus while she slept. Leah felt a stab of fear, being that alone, but she bullied herself out of it. She was hungry. It was almost dark, and usually she'd have eaten dinner at six o'clock.

Leah walked up the dim path from the dorm to the dining hall. Inside, her footsteps echoed loudly, and when she bumped into a chair, the noise made her jump. She was trying to get her phone to work and didn't notice the person who poked his head around the corner from the kitchen.

"Hello?" said the boy.

Leah jumped again and dropped her phone. "Jesus!" she said, looking up at Aidan, a junior she knew only vaguely. "Jesus. You scared the crap out of me."

"Sorry," laughed Aidan. "I thought we were the only ones here."

"We?" asked Leah. She walked into the kitchen and saw two more boys: Travis and Zach, both seniors. They were behind the service bar in the prep area, sitting on the stainless steel counters of the actual kitchen.

Travis waved cheerfully over a huge bowl of cereal. "Help yourself," he called. Zach nodded at her but didn't say anything. He was standing in a dim corner holding a huge knife and using it to cut slices off a block of cheese the size of Leah's thigh.

Leah walked around the edge of the serving counter into the kitchen. It felt weird to be on this side of the counter. Even though she'd gotten food here three times a day, she'd never really noticed the kitchen. Spotting a door to a walk-in freezer, she strolled over and hauled on the door handle. Out came a blast of wet, cold air. After propping the door open for light, she found what she was looking for. It was a five-gallon drum of chocolate peanut butter ice cream. She picked it up and carried it out to a stainless steel counter.

"Awesome!" said Aidan. Leah got a huge mixing bowl and a spoon and served herself a giant pile of ice cream. It had started to soften to the perfect consistency, and she dug out all the little peanut butter cups that she could see. It was amazing.

Travis tossed his cereal in the sink and came over. "Now this is what I'm talking about!" He helped himself to ice cream, and Aidan followed suit. Zach moved away from the cheese and went into the freezer, still carrying the knife. He came out a minute later with some peppermint ice cream, the knife held in his teeth like a pirate.

"So," said Leah over a mouthful of ice cream, "why are you all still here?"

"Why are *you* still here?" asked Zach.

Leah shrugged and swallowed another mouthful of ice cream. "Didn't feel like going home yet."

"Forget going home, man," said Aidan. "This is awesome! We've got this whole place to ourselves. We can eat whatever we want! Do whatever we want. No bells. No check-in. No friggin' pills!"

Travis jumped up on the counter and spread his arms. "We're free!" It echoed weirdly around the cold walls of the kitchen.

Leah sighed. There was no way she was going to spend the next few days with these guys. She finished her ice cream, ignoring the boys as much as possible.

The students at Wiltmore had their own classification system. Each kid had a number. A five meant that you were totally normal but had gotten into really big trouble. Fletcher Roiboson had burned down a wing of his old school as a prank. He was a five. A four meant you could probably act normal if you wanted to, but again you'd gotten into trouble and were on meds to control behavior. A three meant you were on meds and needed them, probably forever. A two meant more than two diagnosed psychological problems and at least one hospitalization. One was Total Wacko, no hope of ever living independently.

Leah thought that Travis and Aidan were probably threes. Severe ADHD, maybe impulse control problems. Zach gave her the creeps. He seemed smart, but careful. Everything he did was a little too polished, so that he came off like someone pretending to be a teenage boy.

"Hey! Look, man! Wine!" Aidan held up a big box of cooking wine.

"That's probably got salt in it," said Leah, but it was too late. Aidan tilted back his head and opened the spout into his mouth. He swallowed a huge gulp and then coughed weakly.

"Ugh. Nasty, bro. Here, you try it." Aidan held out the box to Travis.

Leah waved halfheartedly to the three boys and walked out into the dusky gloom of the dining hall.

She jogged lightly down the staircase outside and turned toward her dorm.

"Leah?"

Leah's heart thudded off beat and she grabbed her chest, locating Mr. Tanden across the green.

"What are you doing here?" Mr. Tanden walked briskly across the grass, frowning.

"Oh, hey, Mr. Tanden." Leah smiled her most reassuring smile.

Mr. Tanden was one of the youngest members of the faculty and the most recently hired. Leah figured he'd gotten stuck with the job of making sure everyone was accounted for. Leah knew him to be a teacher who hadn't gotten too tired to treat each situation as unique. It meant that sometimes he was willing to bend the rules a little. He consulted a clipboard on his way across the grass and stopped in front of Leah.

"This says your folks are picking you up?"

"Yeah, my mom's coming, but she had to drive up from Connecticut." Leah hoped Connecticut was sufficiently far away to explain the delay. "She was visiting my grandmother, but she said she'd be here around ten tomorrow morning."

Mr. Tanden glanced over his shoulder toward his apartment, and Leah guessed he had someone waiting there for him.

"Is your dorm head still here? Ms. Goss?" he asked hopefully.

"No, I don't think so, but I'll be fine. Really." Leah did her best to telegraph confidence straight at Mr. Tanden's head. "I just helped myself to some food in the cafeteria. I hope that's okay. My plan is just to go back to the dorm and sleep, then pack up and meet my mom in the morning."

Mr. Tanden tilted his head and grimaced. Leah almost had him.

"Listen, I'm sure you want to get back to your family as soon as possible," Leah said in her most soothing tone. "I can make it through the night. I can feed myself and I'll be fine in the dorm."

Mr. Tanden dropped his clipboard to his side and sighed with defeat. "I'll probably get fired for this." He laughed humorlessly. "My girlfriend is waiting for me to drive to her folks' house, so . . ." Mr. Tanden sighed again and then straightened. Leah knew he'd leave her alone as long as he didn't find the boys. "Is there anything you need? Anything at all?"

"Nope. Honest, I'll be fine. It's only, like, fourteen hours."

"Right. You'll be fine. Okay."

Leah walked jauntily toward her dorm, feeling Mr. Tanden's eyes and the weight of his concern on her shoulders. She turned suddenly and jogged back to him. "Mr. Tanden?"

"Yes, Leah?"

"I know I just told you that I can take care of myself, but I think I left my key in my room. Could I borrow your keys? For two minutes? I'll just run in, get my key, and come right back out."

Mr. Tanden smiled, and Leah could tell that helping her in this small way was going to make him feel better about the whole thing. He took out a big ring of keys and picked one. "Here, this one should get you in."

Leah grabbed the keys, holding the one Mr. Tanden had picked out. She jogged across the green to her dorm and let herself in. Once inside the door, she went over to a window and picked through the key ring. Each key had two or three letters on it that corresponded with the name of a building. Leah picked out one that said OCS, hoping it meant "Outing club shed." She wrestled it quickly off the key ring and then checked for other useful keys. One said MA. Leah wondered if it meant "master," since there were no buildings on campus that started with *M*. She fumbled that off the key ring and pocketed both keys. She hadn't really left her key in her room, so she waited in the vestibule a bit and tested the weight of the key ring to see if there was a noticeable difference. She couldn't really tell, but hopefully Mr. Tanden would be in too much of a hurry to leave and wouldn't check.

Leah attempted to smooth the guilt off her face and pushed out the door, back to Mr. Tanden. She cheerfully returned the keys, thanked him and wished him luck, then walked back to the dorm.

Inside, she tried the MA key in Ms. Goss's apartment door. It turned easily. Leah realized she could get into any room she wanted. She walked up to the second floor of the dorm, felt along the walls, and opened the first room she came to.

KAILEIGH was written in bubble letters on the door, and inside, the scent of perfume was strong enough to give Leah a headache. Kaileigh was a sophomore, in trouble for selling prescription drugs. Leah opened the shade in the window, and dim light filtered in, sketching the disarray inside. Clothes spilled out of every container, and more shoes than Leah had seen outside a shoe store cascaded from a corner like a colorful landslide. What was Kaileigh doing with five-inch platform shoes in the middle of Maine? Leah picked over the cosmetics that were escaping a plastic tub on the dresser. She chose a silver tube of lipstick and opened it up. Dark purple. Leah put it back. The perfume was getting to her, so she picked her way carefully to the door and left.

Brook lived next door. Her room was also trashed, but fewer clothes and fewer shoes. Brook was at Wiltmore for drunk driving. Driving through storefronts seemed to be her specialty. She'd gone through three on three separate occasions. Brook had a billion gossip magazines and posters everywhere. She was from LA, Leah remembered, and made a big deal about keeping her skin cream in the common-room fridge, where it had a more reliable temperature.

The next room belonged to Eloise Barker, who'd been a mystery to Leah. Rumor had it that she came from a superrich family but had gotten in trouble for stealing really valuable stuff from her Upper East Side friends' homes. After getting caught a few times, she'd finally stolen a priceless sketch by some famous artist—Rembrandt, maybe—but then she'd left it in her bag in the back of a car, and hard candy had melted all over it. Eloise's room was relatively clean. Leah felt a sort of heaviness in the room, as if the things in it were aware of their own worth, as if their value secured them more firmly to the floor.

Leah touched the bed, then sat on it. It was incredible, actually. This definitely wasn't the school-issued mattress. Leah lay back onto the softest sheets she had ever touched and leaned into a mountain of pillows. *So*, thought Leah, *this is what wealth feels like.* The sheets smelled like flowers, not overwhelmingly, like Kaileigh's perfume, but almost like there were real flowers being crushed in the sheets. Leah sighed. Would she be happier, she thought, if she had a bed made of flower-scented clouds? Forty pairs of shoes? Leah thought of the kids at Wiltmore. She knew they were wealthy, almost without exception, but the other thing they had in common, besides the obvious (BIG trouble), was that they all seemed lonely. What money bought you, thought Leah, was the ability to be alone.

Whether you wanted it or not.

44

# Chapter Seven: No More Bagels

## Margot

I woke up and felt nervous right away. I was about to spend the whole morning with Ronan building a smoker, two things I had no idea how to do. I ate a dry, untoasted bagel for breakfast, washed it down with a juice box, and went upstairs to find a shirt that was suitable for chopping up a hickory tree but was also effortlessly sexy.

Ronan and his mom drove up around nine. On Ronan, a white T-shirt was appropriate for chopping up trees and looking effortlessly sexy. His mom helped us squash all the venison into our freezer and then walked back out to their car.

"I had an errand in Lyndonville," she murmured, explaining why she was there too. "I'm just going to read in the car while you two are working," she whispered. "I don't dare waste the gas going all the way back home."

Mom was still sleeping, and I hadn't seen Dad, but I told Mrs. Murphy she was welcome to the living room and anything in our kitchen.

Ronan and I walked to the end of the driveway and a few yards into the woods where the hickory tree was. Ronan expertly chopped down the tree, and then we both attacked it with axes, since that seemed like the best way to get chips. The last thing I wanted to be was some wilting female, so I chopped at that tree for at least an hour before I had to stop and get Band-Aids for some wicked blisters. I walked into the house right as Mrs. Murphy was coming out the front door.

"I just remembered another errand in Lyndon," she said. "I'll be right back." I thought it was weird that Mrs. Murphy, who reminded me of a scuttling mouse, could have produced a son like Ronan.

"Okay," I said. "I'll tell Ronan."

I covered my hands in Band-Aids, grabbed some juice boxes, then went back out to the tree.

Glory be, Ronan had taken off his shirt and was chopping away at the tree with confident, precise swings of the ax.

I coughed and then choked and finally cleared my throat enough to say, "Juice box?"

Ronan leaned the ax up against a tree and toweled off the back of his neck with his T-shirt. I handed him the juice box, and when he accepted it, he grabbed my wrist and inspected my Band-Aids.

I can only describe the sensation as melting. Heat poured from his fingers into my arm and through my whole body.

"Blisters?" he asked.

I shrugged. "Not too bad."

"We need to pick up all these chips. Do you want to do that while I keep chopping?"

I did. We worked out a way for me to pick up chips without getting hacked to pieces by the ax. While we worked, I told him how I'd driven by myself and how I'd wimped out backing up to the gas pump. Ronan laughed and then told me that when he was learning to drive, his dad rode in the car with him for exactly two blocks.

"He screamed these high-pitched little shrieks the whole time," said Ronan, "and when we got to the second stop sign, he just jumped out of the car and walked home."

I imitated my mom trying to figure out which filter to use for her selfies, and pretty soon we were joking around so much I forgot that I was nervous. In about an hour we had two huge buckets of chips. Enough, I thought, to start the fire. We carried the chips to the house just as Mrs. Murphy was getting back from Lyndon. Ronan waved cheerfully at her and she flagged him over. They conferred through the car window for a few seconds, and then Ronan jogged back to me and said he had to go.

"Sorry, Mom says there's something she's got to do and if I want a ride . . ." He shrugged.

"It's all right," I said. "I'll work on getting the meat sliced up and salted. Then I've got to figure out how to hang it. . . ." I trailed off as I realized how much work there was left to do. Plus, the meat was thawing by the minute.

"You know what?" said Ronan. "Do you have a bike I could use?"

"What?"

"If you'll lend me a bike, I could stay and finish this with you."

"Oh," I said. "Yeah, of course. Are you sure, though? You live, like, twenty miles away."

"Nah, it's only ten or so. It'll be great."

"Well, okay. If you want to."

"Gimme a minute," said Ronan.

He jogged back to the car and leaned in his mom's window. She seemed to be arguing with him, but I was busy watching the way Ronan's muscles parted around his hip bone and disappeared into his pants.

It took all day, but we built a smoker that would have done Laura Ingalls Wilder proud. When we saw the smoke, thick and fragrant, curling out of the top of the smoker, I slapped Ronan a high five that turned into a hug. Glory be. We stuck together, kind of, because of the sweat, but I wasn't even embarrassed.

I'd have to keep the fire going for the next week, and Ronan said he'd come back when he could to chop more hickory and then pick up the venison. When I watched him ride away, I felt relief that he wasn't there anymore, taking up all the air, but I missed him almost immediately. I floated inside the house, past Dad, who was freaking out about something, straight up to my room. I lay on my bed just feeling the heat of Ronan all over my front. I couldn't believe it, but sweat could smell really good. I wished I could tell Leah.

I got to enjoy my Ronan-induced coma for a little while longer, but then Mom burst into my room.

"Honey, do you have the cash? The cash I got from the bank?"

I stared at her until I remembered how she'd held her hands apart at the party to show how big the wad of cash had been. It had been big.

"Why? Is it missing?" I asked.

"Oh, no. I'm sure it's not missing." Mom waved away the idea. "I just can't remember where I put it." Mom frowned and swept my room with her eyes. "I was so busy with the party. . . ." Mom trailed off and disappeared down the hall. Served her right, I thought, for bragging about it at the party. It wasn't like there was anything to buy anyway.

We didn't really have dinner that night because Mom and Dad were fighting about Leah and the senator and the cash and whether or not the blackouts were real. Dad used up most of a tank of gas yesterday driving to two different airports, and so he really needed the cash, but it was gone. They were hissing at each other, which I hated, so I went and added more wood to the smoker.

I squatted down next to the smoker and poked the fire with a stick. Should I feel bad for not filling up the car and getting gas, like Grandma asked? Honestly, it was up to Mom and Dad to plan things out a little better, but they weren't exactly inspiring me to confidence. Worry about Leah was like a sweater with a collar that was too tight. Dad and I both had one on, but it seemed like Mom didn't.

I read the rest of the Laura Ingalls Wilder book and shared a box of Triscuits with Lucas on the couch. He was reading a comic book about Lewis and Clark. Lucas too big to really snuggle with anymore but sitting there on the couch together, we got closer and closer until I just put my arm around him. We both pretended we weren't snuggling, but it was really nice to have his little-boy smell right next to me. We had to stop reading when the sun went down, which meant that we had to stop snuggling. Before Luke pulled away he looked up at me and said in a really quiet voice, "I'm worried about Leah."

I kissed the top of his head and talked into his hair. "Me too, buddy." I wished I could tell him that she'd be home tomorrow for sure, but I couldn't, so I squeezed him against my chest.

"Gross," said Luke, squirming out of the hug. "I touched your boob."

# Chapter Eight: 1,996 Miles

### Caleb

It is morning, early morning, I think, because of the mist, and Dad is still asleep. I look around and it turns out that we slept right next to a little dirt road. I don't remember getting here very well, just waking up when the motorcycle stopped. We drove for a long time yesterday, and I tried to stay awake because I didn't want to fall off. Even so, I almost did fall asleep and Dad felt me jerk awake. He pulled over and moved me up between his legs. This is possible because my dad is really big, and even though I am already eleven, I am pretty puny. I take after my mom, I guess, but Dad is always asking if I've had my growth spurt yet. I know it is a disappointment to him to have a shrimp for a son, but he should think how I feel about it.

The highway can't be far away, because I heard it all last night. I can also hear running water nearby. I pick up the two empty Dinty Moore stew cans from our dinner and go find the stream.

It is a small stream and shady, and really pretty with a nice sandy bottom. I rinse out the stew cans without slicing my finger open like I did last year on the Worst Camping Trip Ever and then fill them with clean water. I know better than to drink water out of a stream, so I bring it back to where Dad is still sleeping. I pump up the stove and wait for Dad to wake up. I wait about a minute and then light the stove all by myself. I boil one can of water and set it aside to cool. Since lighting the stove went so well, I decide to try making coffee. I find the coffeepot and grounds and throw a handful in the bottom of the pot. I throw in another handful to be sure and then pour in the other can of water. It is just starting to smell like coffee when Dad wakes up. He looks at the stove and the coffee and the water and then grunts, farts, and goes off to pee. I take it to mean he is proud of me.

I drink some of the water after it has cooled and make oatmeal with the rest. Dad bought the cheap instant kind that is mostly oatmeal dust and sugar. It isn't bad, though it has a distinct beef flavor from the can. Dad takes one sip of coffee and barks like a seal.

"Now that is some coffee, bub! Tell me, have my teeth dissolved?" He grins at me and I smile back. I slurp my oatmeal while Dad drinks his coffee and then his last can of beer. We don't talk much and it is a nice morning.

A little while later and we are driving again. I mean, riding. Dad says you ride a motorcycle, not drive one. Dad gave me some of his coffee with evaporated milk in it, and now I don't know if I feel jittery from that or from being back on the motorcycle again. We stop in some small town for lunch and we buy sandwiches at a little gas station where the owner is sitting at the door with a shotgun across his knee. He warns us that his credit card machine don't work and that the freezers are all off. His wife inside says that folks were looting everywhere on account of the credit card machines not working anywhere. Dad says he's never had a use for credit cards anyway and pays cash. He asks if they have any beer left. She smiles at him like all women do and says no, it was the first thing to go.

Outside Dad asks the man if there's a place nearby to get a beer, and the man says that as far as he knows, Dad's only bet might be in Hinesburg, eleven miles away from the interstate. Then Dad kind of looks at me and shrugs, and I know it's because of me that we don't go and get beer.

Back on the highway, we pass at least three cars that have run out of gas. I am nervous for Mom.

Now it is afternoon and hot. I think it might be Dad who is making me feel hot because his back is like a heater. I wish there was some way to hold on without being so close to him. Suddenly he swerves a bit and the bike wobbles. I grab hard at his sides and we straighten out. Dad is clawing at the front of his jacket. With a *snap*, the jacket opens enough so that the wind fills it with hard air and rips out of my hands. I grab forward and yell and the bike wobbles again. I am pretty scared now, and I try to yell to Dad, but it is too loud. I tug at his arm and he yells something that might be "Just a minute," or it might be "God damn it." I hush and hang on for dear life. We get to an exit and I tug at his arm again. He turns at the last minute and we roar off the highway, then brake hard at a stop sign. Dad sort of falls to one side, but we get our balance again and drive a little bit until we get to a strip of woods by a big field that has a dirt road going along one side. Dad stops the motorcycle, then it takes him three times to hit the kickstand.

"I'm not feeling so good, bud," he yells too loud, fumbling with his helmet and standing sort of funny. "I got to be alone for a few hours, all right?"

I stare at him. He is sweating like someone is pouring a bucket of water down his face, but instead of red, like normal, he is whitish in his face. I don't even say anything, just look at him until he whirls around and stumbles along the edge of the woods, then out of sight.

At first I just stare after him. Then I look out at the road to see if anyone might come along to help us. I see five, six, seven cars pass by on the highway, but nobody comes our way. I wonder if I poisoned him by accident with the coffee, but I had some too and I feel fine now that I'm off the motorcycle. I wonder about the sandwiches, being in a warm cooler, but we went halves on those and Dad didn't eat much. I follow down along the woods to where Dad disappeared. The woods are really just a strip of small trees that have grown up along a ditch where some water is running. I find Dad curled up next to the ditch. He got his jacket off, and his shirt is all dusty, with bits of twigs on it. He rolls toward me, but he looks right through me; his eyes don't even stop when they hit my face. I'd say Dad looks poisoned or really sick, but I can't think of why.

I have to admit that I am pretty mad. I'm mad at my dad for being sick. I'm mad at my grandma for saying we should drive across the country. I'm mad at my mom for not being here and mad at everyone who drives by on the interstate and doesn't stop to help me. I am mad that I am hungry and nobody has even given me a snack since lunch and now it's got to be at least dinnertime.

I realize that this is something I can fix. There are candy bars in my backpack on the trailer. I walk hard back to the bike and trailer and kick one of the tires to show how mad I am. It really is hot even without me hanging on to Dad, and I bet that all our food is melting or something. I let the bungee cords go from around our stuff and carry the trash bag of food off into the shade of the woods. I get my backpack and then decide I should probably get the gas cans, because I am pretty sure that you're not supposed to leave gas where it might get hot and explode. I take the keys, too, because it makes me nervous just to have them in the ignition like that. I bring it all down by the ditch under the trees and sit there for a little bit, eating a candy bar. I am still mad but also I feel good for saving the gas cans from exploding. I hope Dad feels bad that he didn't do it, then I feel bad that I am not taking care of him, because he must be pretty sick.

I walk down the edge of the trees and find Dad again.

"Dad?" I say, really quiet. I can see that he threw up and also he got a little on his jacket.

"Go 'way, buddy." He growls it really soft and sloppy. Just then I hear a car over by where our motorcycle is.

"I'll be right back, Dad," I tell him, and I walk quickly back toward the road. At first I am excited, thinking that someone is here to help, but then I think that maybe whoever it is might not be nice and might be the kind of person who offers kids candy bars to get in their cars with them. So before I get to the end of the woods, I walk really quietly and listen. I hear three guys talking, probably high schoolers.

"Check it out, guys, a bike!"

"Piece-of-crap bike."

"Shove it, man. What's your car get per gallon? Seven miles?"

"Screw you."

"Are the keys in it?"

"Nope, I bet I could jump it, though."

"Bull crap!"

"Well, Marty could."

"Yeah, I bet—didn't we just see his truck outside the garage?"

"Yeah, that was him, all right."

I turn and creep back to my pile of stuff by the ditch. I can hear them talking a little bit more, but not what they're saying. I have to get Dad. I am pretty scared that they will get Marty and he'll steal our bike and we'll be stuck here and never make it to Vermont. Dad needs medicine, I'm pretty sure, but all we have is aspirin. I have the little bottles of Canadian Mist whiskey too and something about them tugs on my brain. I think about in cowboy movies how when they're about to dig a bullet out of someone's leg, they always give the guy a slug of whiskey for a kind of medicine or to make him feel brave. I find one of the tiny bottles.

Dad sucks it down. I mean, actually sucks on the bottle to get every last bit. He sits with his head in his hands for a minute and his back is still and then he looks at me, squinting. Since I can tell that he sees me this time, I tell him about Marty and the high school boys. He gets up after two tries and we go back to the motorcycle. Dad tells me I should call it a bike, not a motorcycle. I guess he really is better. I reload all the stuff and dad sits on the *bike* with his head in his hands. He tells me good job about the gas and then he bungees it all in place.

We drive one more hour and then Dad pulls over and finds a nice spot to camp. I know he is sorry for being sick, even though it's not his fault. He sets out everything for camping in a really nice way and lets me start the stove again. After I eat and he drinks some coffee, he tells me that he's going to get sick again soon and that we'll stay here until he is better, probably tomorrow or the day after. He asks if I can take care of myself and feed myself, and I say yes. He asks if I have any more of the Canadian Mist whiskey, then says never mind, don't tell him, but if there is an emergency and we need to leave, give him one of those.

He says he's sorry for being sick. I say, why? Why is he sick? And he says because, well, never mind, he'll explain when I'm older. That hurts my feelings a little bit, and Dad clomps his big hand on my shoulder and tries to explain how beer makes you sick when you drink it all the time and then stop drinking it all of a sudden. I'm not sure, except I can see he's getting sweaty again, and smelling really bad, so I don't ask any more. Dad tucks me in my sleeping bag even though it is still really light out, and then he goes and curls up in his sleeping bag, away from me. His breathing is really jerky.

I'm going to count all the different birds I can hear until I fall asleep.

# Chapter Nine: Mistake #876

## Leah

After one day of hanging out in the dorm by herself, Leah was becoming mortally bored. She read most of Brook's magazines, tried on everyone's clothes, and found some really great stashes of candy. At noon she watched through her blinds as a car pulled up and an entire family got out. Half an hour later the family came back with Aiden and drove off together. Leah felt a stab of loneliness and checked her phone. Still nothing.

By afternoon she decided to go back to the kitchen and find something healthier to eat. She hoped that she wouldn't see the boys. If she was lucky, she wouldn't see anyone.

She wasn't lucky.

Travis shouted from a corner in the back of the kitchen, "Tortilla chips! Dude, I found chips!"

Leah gave him a smile, then ducked into the fridge. It was room temperature now, but damp and starting to smell like rotting vegetables. She found some unopened cheese in a giant fifteen-pound block. When she went back out into the kitchen, the boys were leaving with the chips.

"We're having a party tonight in Moore's office. You should come!" called Travis.

Leah waved noncommittally and the door slammed shut.

She found some water in a huge aluminum pot on the stove and made pasta. She put big chunks of cheese in it, and it wasn't half bad. Leah looked around at all the food the boys had left out to rot. She had to get out of here.

Leah left the kitchen and plunged once again into the dim light of the dining hall. Only a little bit of dusky light came in through the windows. *I need a light*, thought Leah. Last night she'd gone to bed at dark, mostly out of necessity. The Outing Club shed would have plenty of headlamps, as long as she could get in.

Leah stepped into the waning afternoon and headed toward the north side of campus, where the small Outing Club shed was. When she got there, she peered at the keys she'd stolen. Leah chose the one that said OCS and tried it in the lock. It turned and the shed door swung open, releasing the smell of old woodsmoke and mildew. Leah loved the smell. Some of the few good times she'd had at the school had been on the overnight trips put on to "promote self-esteem and responsibility." The shed was tidy but dirty. The teacher who led the program, Mr. Ford, was organized but believed that it was only natural that hiking equipment would be soot stained and crumbling with dried dirt.

Leah located a rack of headlamps and tried two before she found one that worked. She put that on and then looked around a bit. She found a camp stove and a canister of propane. She checked, and sure enough, there was a lighter that worked inside the stove bag. Up on a shelf were a dozen packets of hot cocoa. Leah decided it might be nice to climb up on the roof of the main building and make cocoa later. She located "her" backpack on the rack of backpacks and stuffed the stove and cocoa inside. She grabbed a Therm-a-Rest, rolled it neatly, and tucked that in too. Feeling cheerful, Leah left the shed, locked it, and headed back toward the main part of campus.

Dusk had crept over the campus and it was cool, though a warm breeze remained as a reminder of the day. Leah's ears strained to pick up signs of life, human life, but there were none. Over in the main building she saw lights bobbing wildly down a hall. She wondered if the boys had actually drunk the salted cooking wine.

Leah made her way over to the admin building to do some snooping. She took out the MA key, hoping it would work, and sure enough, the lock turned. She slipped in the door and passed through the fancy parlor that Admissions used to impress parents. Switching on her headlamp, Leah wandered through a secretary's office and then into a room of file cabinets.

The room was lined on both sides with cabinets that were as tall as Leah. She poked around in a few before she found the cabinets that had the student files. She looked at file labeled "Wainsworth, Pepper." Pepper was a senior girl who was supposed to be a one. Total Wacko. One page listed eight different medications. One drug Leah recognized as an antidepressant, one was a drug for ADHD, and one was birth control. Leah didn't know the other five. She skimmed through four pages of psychological summary on Pepper. Started off with an eating disorder at age eleven, ran away three times when she was twelve, diagnosed with ADHD at age twelve, another eating disorder, hospitalized twice, and a suicide attempt with pills . . . Leah put the file away, feeling guilty.

Leah found her own file and browsed through it. "Her IQ of 156 is extremely high, although she does not seem to live up to her potential. . . Suffers depression after—" Leah slammed the file shut. Leah was a four.

She struggled for a minute to remember Zach's last name and then found his file. His IQ was pretty high too, not as high as Leah's, though. Leah didn't recognize any of his meds except for one study drug. She opened his profile. "Zach can be powerfully charismatic if he chooses to be. He came to us after his previous school discovered he was the head of a club in which all the members had to allow Zach to perform sadistic acts on them in a ritual setting. These acts included nailing the webbing between their fingers to a table, burning a homemade brand on the bottoms of their feet, and one broken arm. It was the broken arm that alerted the school authorities to Zach's club. Zach seems to be incapable of empathy with or even sympathy for his fellow humans. . . ." Leah stopped reading and swallowed. She hadn't known that Wiltmore even had this kind of student. Zach was definitely dangerous. Just to be sure, Leah looked up Travis. He was a three with a long list of meds. Leah closed the files, picked up her backpack, and walked back outside, thoughtful and quiet. She decided to avoid Zach and start making plans to leave. She wondered if her dad was on his way. For the first time since all the lights went out, Leah began to worry about how she was going to get home.

It was nearly dark as she walked back over to the main building. She had to get water, but none of the water fountains were working, so she decided to go to the water jug in the teachers' lounge. She walked down the main hall back toward the kitchen and noticed that there was light leaking out from under the door to the headmaster's office. She turned off her own light and decided to sneak by, but suddenly a terrible scream came from behind the door. Leah froze. Should she try to save whoever it was or just get out of there?

Just then the door burst open and Travis stumbled into the hall. He raced to a big potted tree and vomited into the soil. He turned to face Leah, and she was blinded by his headlamp.

"Hey," he said groggily. "We foun' some rum." Travis gagged again and turned away from Leah, back toward the headmaster's office. "C'mon," he said. "We're doin' brands."

Leah cautiously followed Travis inside the office. Candles were lit around the room, casting a flickering light on the rich, masculine furniture of the office. There was a terrible burned, meaty smell in the room, mixed with another chemical smell. Zach sat on top of the headmaster's desk, holding a thick wire hanger that had been bent into some kind of shape. He had a can of hair spray next to him and a lighter. Travis flopped into a chair, gripping his arm right above the elbow. His head drooped drunkenly, bobbing as he chuckled without mirth. Zach seemed coldly sober. He studied Leah and then shrugged, the look of cold calculation sliding off his face, replaced with a friendly smile.

"Rum?" he asked, holding up a bottle.

"I'm cool," said Leah.

"Aw, c'mon, Leah. Have some. An' then you shou' getta bran' too." Travis jerked his head up with an effort.

"Not my thing, guys," said Leah.

"Not my thing, guys," said Zach in an eerie falsetto.

"Not my thing guys," echoed Travis. "C'mon," he said, lurching to his feet. "It sawesome."

"No way," said Leah. She laughed nervously. "I'll see you guys later." Leah turned toward the door, but Zach stepped in front of her.

"Stay," he said. "Have a drink."

"No," Leah sneered at him and tried to push by, but Zach shoved her. She tripped sideways over a book on the floor and the weight of her pack pulled her onto her side.

"Hold her arms," Zach ordered Travis.

Travis dropped clumsily to his knees by Leah's head and grabbed at her hands. Leah slapped at him and he lost his balance, accidentally kneeing her in the side of the head. A shower of sparks spiraled away in Leah's vision and for a moment sounds were warped and hollow. Leah couldn't even struggle as Travis grabbed both her arms and pinned them to her sides.

Coming back to herself, Leah began to fight in earnest, wrenching one arm free, but the other arm was tangled in her backpack and Travis outweighed her by at least forty pounds. He sat on Leah's hips and tried to grab her arm, and then Zach sat on Leah's head, pining her in a ball on her side. Leah could barely breath and couldn't move at all except to kick her legs uselessly.

"Wait a minute, wait a minute," she panted, shouting up from beneath Zach. "Not my right arm, okay? Not my right arm!" She held still.

"Let her turn over," commanded Zach. "Then roll up her sleeve."

Zach and Travis loosened their grips and Leah got to her hands and knees. Trying to gather her wits, she paused and then kicked at Travis and launched herself over Zach. Zach grabbed her around the waist, and Travis wrenched her leg so hard that the pain knocked the breath out of her lungs. She was momentarily dazzled, inert, so the boys rolled her roughly onto her side and sat on her again.

Leah's chest heaved, trying to catch her breath. Finally she managed a sip of air. She screamed then as loud as she could, but who was there to hear her?

Leah saw a flash of light, and out of the corner of her eye she watched as Zach ignited a plume of hair spray, then held the bent wire in the flame to heat it up. He held it there until the wire was red hot and glowing.

"Hold her still," he said, looking with fascination at the glowing wire. He put the lighter and the hairspray on the desk behind him and approached Leah with a manic grin.

Leah screamed with every last bit of breath she had and then realized someone else was yelling too.

A burst of flame briefly haloed Zach's head. Bands of fire passed over Travis, and the boys rolled away from Leah. Leah scrambled to her hands and knees and crawled toward the door. Another blast of flame roared over her head.

"Nobody move!" A boy was there, holding the can of hair spray with the lighter lighted in front of it. He pressed down on the nozzle and another plume of fire swept into the room, keeping Leah's captors where they were on the floor.

Leah scrambled back to the door and opened it while the boy backed toward her. She held the door for him until his foot could prop it open.

"Hold them for one second," panted Leah. She ran across the hall and knocked over the potted tree. Her panic gave her strength, so, gasping, she rolled the pot across the hall.

"Come on," she yelled. The boy darted into the hall and let the door close. Together they rolled the potted tree against the door and propped it upright. Already someone was pounding on the other side.

"This way!" gasped Leah. She and the boy ran down the hall and back across campus to her dorm. The beam from the boy's headlamp bobbed crazily across the grass in front of them, so that shadows leaped at them from every direction. Shaking, Leah found the master key and opened the front door of her dorm. The boy turned to go upstairs to the students' rooms, but Leah pulled him back.

"In here," she said. Using the master key, she opened Ms. Goss's apartment. They both fell inside and Leah slammed the door behind them. "Turn off that light," she panted. He did and the apartment was pitch dark.

They both sat there in the dark, trying to catch their breath as quietly as possible and straining to hear if they'd been followed. Slowly Leah's eyes adjusted to the lack of light. She sat up shakily and peered at her rescuer.

"Holy crap," she said.

It was the senator's son.

Leah started to laugh.

"What?" said the boy.

Leah cackled harder and the boy laughed nervously.

"It's just . . . ," Leah gasped helplessly.

The boy leaned back and stared at Leah skeptically. "I thought you were, like, a four or something. Are you crazy?" He meant it literally, and that made Leah laugh even harder.

"No, no." Leah coughed into her hand and giggled. "I told my mom that—well, never mind. It's a long story. What are you doing here? I thought you'd be the first one out of here. Didn't your dad give everybody the heads-up about the blackouts? You'd think they'd be more careful with a senator's kid."

The boy sneered at her. "You don't know anything."

Leah shrugged, agreeing. "Well, thanks for, uh, back there."

The boy stopped sneering and shrugged. "That guy's a creep."

"Yeah."

They looked at each other for a minute in silence.

"So," said Leah. "What's your name?"

"Sam." The boy looked a little miserable in the dim light.

"Hi, Sam. I'm—"

"Leah. I know your name."

Leah felt sorry for him for some reason, and guilty that she hadn't known his name. "I didn't really feel like going home yet," she offered.

"Me neither."

"I don't really want to stick around with Hannibal Lecter here, though."

"I was gonna . . . ," Sam started to say, and then stopped. "I'm gonna hike on the Appalachian Trail for a little while."

Leah saw that it was an invitation.

"Sounds good to me."

# Chapter Ten: Last Cinnamon Roll

## Margot

The next morning I found Grandma in our kitchen organizing things and unpacking food into our cupboards. I gave her a hug, and she handed me a big cinnamon roll on a plate. It was kind of stale, but still better than the dry bagel I'd eaten yesterday.

"When did you get in, Grandma?"

"Last night. Late," she said, trying to find a spot for a big bottle of oil. "I had to drive about forty miles an hour the whole way, since there's stuff abandoned on the highway."

"Really? Why?"

"Folks ran out of gas, tried to carry some things, and gave up. Everyone's trying to get out of the cities or up to Canada. Soon the highway's going to be totally blocked," she said. "I sent your dad out after Leah. Gave him four hundred bucks in cash, told him to find some gas and get going!"

I was so relieved that finally a real grown-up was in charge, even though the news about the highways seemed ominous. I showed Grandma all the stuff in the basement that Lucas and I had bought. She was really happy about it, and I was glad it didn't have to be my fault or a secret anymore.

I told her about our smoker, and she frowned intently the whole time she was listening. Finally she nodded once. "Good thinking, Margot. Those Little House books could be a gold mine."

We went back up into the kitchen, and Grandma showed me a list of things we had to do to get ready for winter. "Really, Grandma?" I said, pointing to number three: *Plant root crops and dig cold storage.*

Grandma glared at me over the top of her glasses. "Are you just going to wait for someone to rescue you? You think the government is going to wave a wand and all this will get better?"

I held up my hands in surrender, but Grandma pointed her finger at me.

"You know that I just drove through three states and there wasn't electricity or cell service anywhere? People walking along the highway like refugees, and these are rural places we're talking about! Think of the people on the fortieth floor of a building in New York City! What if they're in a wheelchair? How long before Boston runs out of food? Or water? Whoever did this managed it all in a matter of hours. Can you imagine what it would take for somebody to pull that off? The entire Internet has, for all intents and purposes, just disappeared! Do you think that our bank records are safe? Social Security?"

I sat down hard at the kitchen table and looked up at my grandmother, whose jowls were wiggling with the force of her lecture. The meaning of her words began to penetrate slowly, but my brain resisted the idea of a total disaster.

"Well," I said lightly. "Guess I better go check on the smoker, then." I shot out of the kitchen before Grandma could yell at me anymore.

I thought about what Grandma had said and realized that things might not go back to normal for at least a month or maybe even two, assuming someone was working to get it sorted right now. What if no one was trying to fix it? What if whoever had caused the blackouts was planning something worse? I'd feel better when Leah was home, I told myself. I'd feel better when someone told us what was really happening.

I had to restart the smoker fire, but it was still warm and smoky inside, so I was pretty sure the meat was still okay. I got the fire crackling and then tossed in more chips, watching with satisfaction as the smoke pouring out the top turned thick and gray.

I needed more information about what was happening and I knew who would have it. I hopped on my mom's bike, since Ronan had mine, then me and my Slinky boobs biked down the hill toward Judy's house.

Here's the funny part: I was almost there when I saw Judy, and I knew she was biking to my house.

"Judy!"

"Go-Go!" Go-Go is the nickname Judy gave me when we were two. Now the whole softball team calls me that, but it's still the best coming from her. We got all tangled up in our bikes trying to hug each other, and laughed. We started talking at once and ended up shouting and grinning, then hugging again.

"Okay," said Judy. "I'll come to your house and look at your smoker, but I get to talk first." I turned my bike around, and we started the long ride back up the hill. Panting, Judy told me that her family was the only one out of ten families on her road that had water because they had some kind of special well that didn't use electricity.

"Everyone has been coming to our house now, to get water," she said. "We keep hearing all this crazy stuff. Last night a whole block of houses burned down in Saint Johnsbury because somebody tried to cook something in their fireplace."

I was surprised. House fires seemed sort of old fashioned, something you worried about when you used to want to be a firefighter.

"Plus, the hospital has all these generators, but they're going to run out of gas soon, so they're trying to figure out what to do with all the sick people."

"Jeez," I said.

"Hey, do you guys have water?"

I told Judy about Luke's spring and how my dad was trying to figure out our well. "He thinks he can put a handle on it somehow so that we can pump it the old fashioned way, but I don't know. We just turn on the generator in the morning and fill up a bunch of jugs of water. Dad's not going to figure it out today, though—he's supposed to go get Leah, and he's got to find gas first."

When we got back to my house, Grandma was standing in the kitchen surrounded by stacks of food boxes and towers of cans.

"I'm doing an inventory of food so we know how to ration," said Grandma, giving Judy an absentminded hug. "Your mom is awake. . . ." Here Grandma made a fluttering motion with her hand. "She's mad at me for not believing her senator story, and she can't find a big wad of cash." Grandma took a deep breath and peered over her glasses at Judy. "But how are you, Judy? How's your family?"

Judy shrugged and looked around. When she spotted the towers of food she frowned. "Good, I guess," she said. "But we're not, like, doing *this*." She pointed at Grandma's inventory. "We have water, though. So that's good." Judy didn't look sure.

"You have water?" Grandma put on her glasses and made a note on her clipboard.

I could tell that Grandma was freaking Judy out, so I grabbed Judy's arm and dragged her out to the smoker.

"Your grandma's really taking this whole thing pretty seriously, huh?"

"Yeah, but at least she got Dad to go get Leah."

"Your mom's nuts, you know."

"Oh, I know." I laughed a dry laugh. "She threw this stupid Blackout Blowout Party and bragged to everyone about how much cash she got out of the bank, but now it's missing, so probably one of her so-called friends stole it."

Judy looked impressed by all the drama, so she only made fun of me a little bit about the smoker. She watched me add some more chips and fuel to the fire while I told her every little detail about Ronan.

"You should throw *all* those chips into the fire so that Ronan has to come back and chop more wood." Judy grinned at me, and just the mention of Ronan's name hollowed out my gut.

Judy saw the look on my face and pushed my shoulder, which knocked me over, since I was still squatting in front of the smoker. I threw a stick at her from the ground and she tossed a handful of leaves at me, screaming. I threw leaves at her, and then Lucas came up and gave us one of his *looks*, which made us laugh even harder. The blackout stuff, the hospitals, no water, missing cash and no Leah all seemed far away as we sat there picking leaves out of each other's hair.

"It's not so bad, right?" Judy asked, looking out into the woods.

"Nah," I said. "If things go south, you can always come live with us. Grandma's getting us ready for Armageddon."

Judy nodded but didn't smile. "My folks aren't that worried," she said. "But maybe they should be. I don't know."

"What are people saying?" I asked.

70

"Nothing. Everything. Everybody's got a theory. Nobody has been killed yet. No bombs or anything. So maybe it's not terrorists."

"They're just letting us get weak first," I said in a bad Terminator accent.

"A couple people say that it's because of the president. People hate him so much and he didn't even win the popular vote, so it's like a rebellion or a coup."

"Whoa," I said, considering. "Could've been an environmentalist group, though, too," I offered. "Anyone who has a solar panel still has power, right?"

Judy shrugged at me and then said, "At least you'll have a boyfriend to keep you warm if we have to, like, go back to the ice ages or something." Judy poked me in the side.

I grinned.

"I better go back home and see if anyone's given any thought to our survival," said Judy dramatically.

"Save them from themselves, Judy," I said.

"Mom's going to run out of coffee soon, then she'll get serious. She had to grind it with a mortar and pestle this morning."

I waved Judy down the driveway and then went back inside and helped Grandma with the inventory. We stacked a bunch of cans in the dining room, since we never used it, and we were running out of room in the kitchen. Grandma had brought tons of food up from Connecticut. It looked like enough food to last until Christmas to me, but Grandma frowned and muttered the whole time.

We'd just started on the boxes of food when the doorbell rang, and it made us both jump.

I went to the door, and when I saw that it was Ronan, I felt that electric shock, followed immediately by the strong suspicion that I still had leaves in my hair.

"Hey," I said.

Ronan's mouth twitched like there was a grin trying to escape, but I noticed that his face was white and sweaty and there were two pink spots high up on his cheeks that looked like thumbprints. "Hey," he said. Then he cleared his throat. "Is your mom here?"

I was so surprised that it took me a minute to figure out what he'd said. "My mom?"

"Yes." Ronan swallowed visibly. "I have to talk to her."

"Oh." I paused, my mind spinning without producing a single usable thought. I stepped to the side to let him in, then stared at his profile as he passed. Was he mad at me? He seemed more nervous than mad. What had my mom done this time? I felt a cold stab of worry work its way into my spine.

"Mom?" I called. Grandma pointed upstairs, so I went and shouted up the stairwell, "Mom, Ronan Murphy's here to talk to you!" I heard movement upstairs, then turned back to Ronan. "She'll be down in a minute," I said, talking like we'd never spoken before. Ronan grinned at me briefly and I melted a bit. I tried to think of something to say, but there was absolutely nothing coming from my brain. I waved around the kitchen.

"Inventory," I said.

"What?" said Ronan.

For probably the first time in recent history, I was happy to see my mom.

"Hello, Ronan," she said breezily. I studied her for a clue as to what this was about.

"Uh, Mrs. Deford." The pink spots on Ronan's cheeks turned bright red. "Can I talk to you for a minute?" Ronan

72

looked at me and Grandma and frowned. I shrank back into the dining room, and Grandma huffed in after me. I carefully restacked some cans, then accidentally knocked over a huge tower. All the noise made it impossible to eavesdrop on the next room. If it is possible to sprain your ears, I did.

After about five minutes I heard the front door open and close again, so I rushed into the kitchen. Mom was alone, frowning. I hesitated a second and then ran out the front door. Ronan was walking down the driveway with his hands in his pockets.

"Hey," I said, jogging up. "Is everything okay?"

Ronan stopped and grimaced. "No," he growled, "it's my mom."

"*Your* mom? Usually it's *my* mom who makes people look like you do right now."

Ronan raised his head and winced through his bangs. "Yeah, well, this time it's my mom." Ronan kicked at the dirt in the driveway and looked uncertain.

"You wanna go check the smoker?" I offered. I was spending way more time with the smoker than I had anticipated.

Ronan nodded and followed me into the woods without speaking. At the smoker, he plopped himself on the ground and tossed a few wood chips into the fire.

"You know how your mom told everyone about the cash from the bank?"

"Yeah."

"Yesterday, before we got here, my mom tried to get cash from the bank, but they were closed."

I waited.

"They even had this scrawny guy with a uniform and a gun making sure people didn't try to break in." Ronan puffed up his cheeks and blew. For a second, with his cheeks all round and chubby, he didn't look so perfect. It was kind of nice.

"I have this problem. It's a disease called Crohn's disease, and I have to really watch what I eat, and take medication that helps me digest my food."

I nodded and started pulling apart a leaf.

"My medication is super expensive."

"So your mom took the money from my mom to buy your medicine," I said quietly.

Ronan looked surprised and then ashamed. "Yeah. Usually insurance pays for the medicine, but since computers are down . . . My mom's super worried that I'm going to run out before this whole thing gets fixed, so she bought as much of my prescription as she could. Basically, it was everything they had, and she had to pay cash. Your cash."

I nodded again and looked at Ronan. "Did you get enough?"

Ronan shrugged. "I've got about four months' worth now, but if things look bad, I can maybe spread it out a little."

"What happens if you don't have the medicine?"

"Basically, my intestines start bleeding and I starve to death." Ronan attempted a grin, but it failed pretty miserably.

I stood up and offered him my hand. "I'm glad you got your medicine," I said.

Ronan looked up at me and then grabbed my hand, hauling himself into standing position.

"Really?"

"Really."

Somehow, when I said "Really," what I truly said was *I like you.*

"Thanks, Margot," said Ronan. It was *just* possible that "Thanks, Margot" meant *I like you, too.*

74

"I offered your mom all the venison," said Ronan. "So I really hope this smoker works. I also said I'd work to help pay you guys back if the banks don't open soon."

"Do you think that this is real?" I asked. "Like, we're in survival mode?"

"I don't know. Could happen, right?"

"My grandma wants to dig a root cellar and plant crops for the winter." I laughed to show I didn't quite think things were that extreme, but Ronan nodded thoughtfully.

"The stores are totally out of food already. Everybody panicked, I guess, and bought as much as they could. My mom, who's like, '*Organic or die,*' came home with twenty cans of supermarket-brand green beans."

"You should see all the food Grandma brought."

Ronan nodded again. "I guess it's good we did this, then, huh?" he said, gesturing to the smoker.

I smiled. "I was sort of embarrassed about it at first."

"No," said Ronan. "It's awesome!" Suddenly he grinned. "Best pickup line ever. 'Bring your meat'!"

I groaned. "I was hoping you didn't remember that."

"I'm glad I did."

The blood sizzled in my cheeks and I had to study the fire so that I didn't have to look at Ronan too closely when I said, "Me too."

# Chapter Eleven: 1,547 Miles

## Caleb

I wake up and check on Dad, but he's not moving, so I lie still for as long as I can stand it, waiting for him to wake up. After a long time I sit up. Dad still isn't moving, but he's breathing loud and raspy, so I know he is alive.

I don't know what time it is, but I'm hungry, so I dig around in the garbage bag and find two packets of oatmeal. This time we're camped pretty far off the road. Dad drove the motorcycle slowly over a dry meadow and parked it under a circle of big trees. We got water last night from a small trickle of a stream that had pockets of mucky water. Dad said to be sure to boil it extra long, so that's what I do now.

I make oatmeal for me and coffee for Dad, in case he wakes up. The oatmeal seems stickier than normal or something, because I can barely swallow. I realize I am scared. Really scared.

I creep over to Dad and nudge him with my foot because I'm holding the coffee in both hands. Dad groans.

"Coffee, Dad," I tell him.

Dad groans again and levers himself up into a sitting position. I kneel carefully in front of him and hand him the coffee. Dad takes a sip without barely opening his eyes. For two seconds I think that everything is going to be okay and we'll be on our way to Vermont soon. Then Dad pukes, just like they do in the movies, which means straight out and all over everything. We are not going anywhere.

I go sit on my sleeping bag, away from Dad and the puke smell. It doesn't take long before the flies find the puke, and if there's anything grosser than puke, it's flies in puke. I can't stop looking at it, and I'm getting madder and more grossed out by the second, so finally I drag Dad's sleeping bag away from him and find a stick to wipe off the puke. Dad's shoes got puked on too, so I drag those away and scrape them down too. A little chunk falls inside the shoe and I leave it in there. I am so mad at Dad. I'm so mad I decide to eat all the rest of the candy bars, which turns out to be only two melted Baby Ruths. As I'm eating, I notice that my hands smell like puke, so I go to the stream to wash, but like I said, it's only a sluggish stream in between mud pots. I try to wash, but I can't get the smell off, and I'm sorry to say this, but I cry for a while.

The day trickles by. Dad wakes up again and drags his sleeping pad into the shade. He takes another sip of the coffee, which has been sitting there forever, and this time he pukes not like in the movies. He's on his hands and knees, and it's like there's an invisible belt yanking up on his stomach. Thick yellow drool oozes out from between his lips. He crawls a little bit away and lies down again.

I make a small tepee of sticks in the shade and then keep adding to it with bigger and bigger sticks. After a while it is taller than me, and I think that if something really bad happens, I will light it on fire like a signal and hope someone comes to get me. I pray to my mom. I ask her to please come take care of me.

There is nothing in the bag I really feel like eating, just more beef stew and some canned corn. It's getting cooler again when Dad sits up and asks for water. I make him some, boiling it extra long, and when it cools off a little, he takes a sip, swishes it around in his mouth, and spits it out. He does that every few minutes and then drinks some. I wait for him to puke, but instead he lies down and goes to sleep again.

Dad doesn't move for a long time, and I can't hear him breathing anymore. I put my fingers on his neck, like they do, and he moves away, so I know he is still alive. The sun goes down and it's instantly cold. I cover up Dad with his pukey sleeping bag. I open the canned corn and eat about half of it. Even though I'm really hungry, I can't eat more. My stomach is being squeezed by the same invisible belt that got Dad. It has been the worst day of my life. I close my eyes before it is even dark and wait to fall asleep.

# Chapter Twelve: Mistake #877

## Leah

When Leah woke up, she stared at the unfamiliar ceiling for a minute and then rolled over on the couch to check if Sam was awake. He was. Leah got the impression that he'd been awake for a while, waiting for her to move before getting up. As soon as he saw she was awake, he jumped up from the floor next to her and started repacking his sleeping bag and air mattress.

"Morning," said Leah awkwardly.

"Morning."

Leah stood and stretched, letting the blanket drop to the floor. Sam avoided looking at her, so she went to the bathroom, and when she came out, Sam was all packed up.

"So, we need to get you some gear," said Sam. Leah appreciated that he was trying to take charge, but his words sounded more like a question than a command.

"I've got the key to the Outing Club shed," said Leah. "I had a backpack and Therm-a-Rest and stove with me in the main building, but I think maybe we should avoid Zach and Travis."

"That guy's a creep," said Sam fiercely.

Leah nodded. "Hopefully, they're either still passed out or sobered up enough not to be psychos."

"Still," said Sam, "I don't want them coming with us."

Leah nodded again, but she thought that it was unlikely that Zach or Travis would want to follow Sam into the wilderness.

They searched Ms. Goss's apartment, and with a touch of guilt they took pasta, jars of sauce, some instant rice, cheese, and oatmeal. It was not a very appetizing collection of food, until Sam found Ms. Goss's chocolate stash in a drawer by the sink. It was extensive and they felt giddy, packing three pounds of chocolate into Sam's pack.

When it was time to go to the Outing Club shed, nervousness crept up Leah's arm from the doorknob. What if Zach was waiting outside to attack them? She inched the door open and peered all around but didn't see anybody. She opened the door wider and checked around farther. Nothing moved, so she stepped cautiously outside and took two steps. Still nothing. Sam followed, tripping on the step and crashing into her. They ran around the back of the dorm to the Outing Club shed and stood panting on the steps, waiting for Leah to get the lock open.

Inside, Leah picked out a sleeping bag, a sleeping pad, a backpack, two water bottles, a headlamp, and a water filter. They divided up the weight of the tent and the food as best they could, then tested their loads. The packs were heavy and they didn't have water yet.

They walked cautiously across campus to the younger boys' dorm to try to find food in Mr. Tanden's apartment. Even though there was definitely plenty of food still in the dining hall, they'd decided not to risk running into Travis and Zach.

Mr. Tanden's fridge had expired milk, condiments, and beer. They found pasta and sauce and protein powder that promised to build muscles, so they took that. Leaving seemed daunting, so they drank one of the warmish beers and stood, burping, by the door.

"Now," said Sam, "we steal a car."

Outside the dorm, the whole campus was still.

"You don't know how to hotwire a car, do you?" asked Leah.

"I was hoping you would."

Leah snorted. "How far is it to the trailhead?"

Sam frowned. "I don't know. Fifteen to twenty miles?"

Leah scanned the campus again.

"Let's take a golf cart," she said, thinking aloud. "They take any key. Security uses them. There should be one around here somewhere."

Sam and Leah looked around the lawn for a golf cart, then walked cautiously out to the main green. There was an abandoned cart right inside the gate, just waiting there for them.

Something made the hair on the back of Leah's neck prickle, so she broke into a trot. Sam started jogging too, and when they reached the cart, Leah looked over her shoulder. Zach was standing on the front steps of the main building with his hands behind his back. He looked down and wiped something off the bottom of his shoe.

"Where's Travis?" Leah whispered, panting.

"Just drive," said Sam.

Leah started the golf cart. She turned to look one last time at Wiltmore.

Zach stood like a menacing statue. He watched them buzz away out the gate and down the road.

# Chapter Thirteen: Newspaper

**Margot**

There was a light drizzle tapping on my window when I woke up in the morning. For a minute I lay there enjoying the soothing sound and the soft light that seeped in through my window. Then, like a gun going off in my ear, the thought of the smoker fire blasted into my head. In less than a minute I went from enjoying the sleepy warmth of my sheets to charging through the woods in my raincoat, getting whacked in the face and shins by wet branches.

When I got to the smoker, the fire was out, and I could see moisture darkening the inside of the tree. All the wood I had stacked next to the smoker was dark and dripping with rain, and the hickory chips were floating in the bucket.

"Dang!" I shouted to no one. "Damn!" Both words seemed equally weak.

I charged back up the hill to the house. There was only one damp piece of newspaper left, so I had to grab a handful of the computer paper from the printer. In the garage I found some dry logs stacked by the door and scooped up as many as I could carry. I got two steps out the door before I remembered a lighter. "Dang!" I shouted again.

It took me the better part of an hour to get the fire roaring. Steam billowed out the top of the smoker and lifted lazily from the muddy knees of my pajama pants. I stood there in front of the smoker with my heart thudding and my backside freezing. What a difference, I thought, between *believing* something and *acting* like you believed something. I had *believed* that the blackouts were a long-term problem and had even made the smoker, but until I had to fight for the smoker, I guess I'd thought that we'd be just as fine without it. It had been something to do, not a vital part of our survival. The realization that this smoker and the meat inside might keep my family from starving at some point thudded into my chest with an audible impact.

I huffed out a breath and bent over at my waist.

"Dang," I whispered.

It rained until midmorning and I babysat the smoker the whole time. When the rain stopped, I brought more dry wood from the garage and covered it with a tarp. I drained the hickory chips in a sieve and laid them out on trays on the back porch to dry. Just that little bit of carelessness, not taking time to cover things, had cost me a whole morning and maybe the food in the smoker. Old Laura Ingalls hadn't said anything about a wet smoker, but Grandma thought that as long as the meat dried out completely, we should be fine.

I was headed back to the smoker, after eating a can of beans for lunch, when Judy shouted at me from the driveway.

"Go-Go!"

I turned and ran up to Judy, waited until she got off her bike, and then crushed her in a hug. We hugged all the time, but this hug was different. This hug was a little desperate.

"What happened?" asked Judy.

83

"The smoker," I said. "The rain put the fire out and the wood was wet and I got . . . I got scared."

Judy hugged me again and talked over my shoulder.

"Somebody threatened my dad with a gun last night."

I didn't say "What!" or make a big deal like I would have before. I just squeezed her again.

"Our well water ran out and Dad had to turn people away. One guy—you know, he lives on the corner and has, like, a hundred dogs? He got really mad that there was no water and yelled at my dad. He said my dad was lying, and then he pulled out a gun and made Dad show him how no water was coming out of our taps anywhere in the house."

Judy pulled away and swiped at her face. "We might leave. My mom wants to go up to our camp on the lake because there's a solar panel there, and a woodstove and an outhouse."

"No!" I said. "I need you here with me!"

"I know." Judy swiped at another tear. "But you didn't see that guy, Margot. He was, like, crazy."

We walked down to the smoker in silence.

"Are you leaving soon?"

"I don't know. At least the rain might fill up our well again."

"Huh," I said.

"Yeah," said Judy. She puffed out a long breath. "Oh, hey." She straightened up suddenly. "I got invited to go hang out with a bunch of people tonight. You should come."

"Really? Where? Who invited you?"

Judy grinned at me. "Madison Hanley invited me to go hang out on I-91."

"The interstate highway? Madison Hanley?"

"I know!" Judy wiggled her eyebrows. "We're meeting on the southbound ramp for exit twenty-two." Judy brushed imaginary dust off her shoulders.

"Explain this," I demanded.

"Well," said Judy in a rich-person accent, "my dear friend Madison came by with her father this morning. Her dad wanted to talk with my dad about actually *selling* our water. He offered to be in charge of security." I shook my head in disbelief but motioned Judy to go on with the story. "So she told me that last night kids from the high school met up and went walking along the highway. Some of the football team found a car with all the windows open and the keys in the ignition. I guess there was some junk food and a bunch of old-school CDs and the car battery still worked, so they had this party out there around the car."

"So, what? There's no traffic out there or something?"

"No. Madison said most people are headed north, to Canada, and everybody has to drive really slow anyway because of all the junk on the road."

"Wow," I said. "Sounds pretty cool."

"I know, but freaky, right? Like, people are just abandoning their stuff."

"They're really that desperate."

"I know."

I tried to explain to Judy what I'd figured out when I was wrestling with the smoker fire.

"All the stuff I was doing before—building the smoker, Grandma's inventory, the garden stuff—it was all just kind of entertainment, you know? I got to hang out with Ronan Murphy, for Pete's sake! But standing out there in the rain, freezing? That was real."

"I know," said Judy. "The guy. The gun."

We looked at each other, and I thought how grown-up Judy looked when she wasn't smiling.

"So, are we going?" I asked.

"Yeah," said Judy. "Heck yeah."

After Judy left, I found Grandma in the kitchen. She had her seed packets out in front of her and was sketching a plan for a garden.

"Hey, Grandma," I said.

"Hey, Sweet Pea." Grandma looked tired, and for the first time I understood how worrying can wear you out. I walked around behind her and hugged her shoulders, resting my chin on her head.

"I have some ideas," I said.

"Oh yeah?" Grandma patted my forearm absentmindedly.

"We should go to some antique stores and see if there's anything helpful, like a hand-crank coffee grinder or a pump, like Dad was talking about."

Grandma put down her pencil and I sat down next to her.

"We could go to the recycling center too and get glass jars for storing food or water. Newspaper, because it helps for lighting fires. Plus, the library probably has books about canning food—"

"Or how to salt it or pickle it!" Grandma was really paying attention now.

"And hunting maybe? Like how to clean out the guts and stuff."

My mom walked into the room, quietly, not like she had a spotlight following her. "We could organize clinics, you know. Find someone who knows how to do all that stuff and then teach it to people." My mom spoke slowly, as if she was actually thinking about what she said. "You know," she said, "we need a

86

way to send messages and spread news. I wonder if we can get radios and broadcasters to work again. Maybe batteries . . ."

Grandma nodded. Mom smiled a hollow smile and spoke softly. "Maybe somebody's seen your father and Leah. If we just put up a notice . . ."

I studied my mother. She hadn't put on makeup, and it made her look ghostly and poorly defined, but the real difference was internal. The brassy light that usually made her seem gaudy and fake had been extinguished. A gentler glow was there now. My mom, for the first time in my memory, was real.

Grandma saw it too. Moving slowly, as if she might scare her daughter away with a sudden movement, Grandma put her hand carefully over my mother's. "They'll come home soon," she said firmly. "I like your idea, though. Let's put up a notice at the post office. One about how to garden and one about Alan and Leah."

"All right, then," said Mom, straightening up. "Let me go put on my face and we'll hit the town!" Just like that, Sparkle Mom was back.

Mom, Grandma, and I drove to three different antique stores in Lyndonville. The first place was closed, and the second place was only trading for gas. The third store looked closed, but it turned out that the couple who owned it lived upstairs. They seemed surprised we were shopping for antiques, but when we explained what we were looking for, they got really excited.

"All this stuff was made before folks had electricity!" said the man, gesturing to his wares. "We'll put out a sign!"

We managed to buy three old-fashioned lanterns and some kerosene, a washboard and a wringer for squeezing water out of wet clothes, and a big washtub. We found a file for sharpening tools and, my favorite, a giant old crosscut saw. We got some

87

hand drills and handsaws and some little metal boxes Grandma said were for warming your bed in the winter. We found the faucet and handle of an old-fashioned water pump, even though none of us knew how we'd attach it to the well. We were able to pay cash for everything, and the guy even gave us a discount because he was so pleased to realize that his antiques might come in handy should the blackout last.

Driving about, we saw a few other cars on the road, plus some that had been left off to the side, maybe run out of gas. A couple of folks had put out signs in their front yards.

DIG YOUR LATRINE FOR FOOD.

ELECTRICIAN. WILL REWIRE YOUR SOLAR PANELS.

NURSING MOTHER WITH EXTRA MILK.

It seemed like we were not the only people to believe that the blackout was serious and possibly long term. It made me feel nervous to be driving the car, seeing as we were probably using up the only gas we had for the foreseeable future.

At the post office we found that the post office box area was open and somebody had put up a huge bulletin board. Already it was covered with lists and advertisements.

The older man who lived next door to the post office had taken it upon himself to be in charge of relaying news. He sat on a lawn chair under a big umbrella and spoke around an unlit pipe to the small crowd.

"A food truck arrived in Saint Johnsbury this morning," he said. "Semi. Big refrigerated thing. Heard it was a mob scene. People crushing one another, pushing, yelling. They didn't even try to unload the truck into the grocery store. The driver fired a gun into the air and then forced everyone into a line and made everyone take only five things each, cash only."

"So it's rations now?" asked Grandma.

"Not officially and it's not organized yet. People with big families were getting the same amount as people shopping just for themselves, and some families had more than one person shopping, so they got twice as much."

"Any trucks coming to Lyndonville?" asked a guy who worked in the bike shop.

"Not that I heard," said the old man. "But I hear the restaurant up the hill is selling off their perishables, cash or trade."

"Anyone know what they're doing over at the prison?" asked a middle-aged man. "I'll bet they've got a lot of food stored up."

"What about the prisoners?" accused a mother with a young boy.

The man shrugged. "Good folks are going to go hungry soon."

"The poor, the imprisoned, the addicted, the old." My grandmother ticked off her list on her fingers. "They will be the first to go. You think anyone is accepting food stamps now? The methadone clinic is still open? You think *everyone* could afford to stock up before the grocery stores ran out of food? And after they're gone, you know what's next to go, don't you? Women's rights."

"We should do something!" said my mom. "I'll organize a food bank. Right here. We just need to collect donations!"

Mom looked eagerly around the crowd.

"Not from me, you won't," said the old man with the pipe. "I got family to see to." He jutted out his chin, and I heard murmurs of agreement from the crowd.

"You do too, Karen," said Grandma. "You want to help people, teach them how to do things for themselves, but don't you go around giving away our food."

89

Mom looked daggers at her mother. "I'll set up a water safety clinic right now," she said defiantly.

Grandma nodded. "Why don't you make a sign. I can teach a class about gardening tomorrow morning."

The woman with the toddler stepped forward. "I can do first aid. Teach a class, I mean. I was a nurse before I had this guy."

Mom beamed at her. "You two go on up the hill," she said, making a shooing motion at me and Grandma with her hand. "I'll walk up when I'm finished here."

Grandma looked at Mom, and I think she was searching for signs of the real Mom we'd seen earlier. Mom twittered her fingers at us and Grandma sighed.

"Come on, Sweet Pea," she said. "Let's go raid the recycling center."

# Chapter Fourteen: 1,547 Miles

### Caleb

When I wake up, before I open my eyes, I get that feeling that someone is looking at me. It's Dad, and he's sitting next to my head. When he sees that I'm awake, he wipes his eyes and then leans over and kisses my forehead.

"We're going to be okay, buddy," he tells me. I don't know if I believe it or not, but it feels so nice to hear it that I go back to sleep.

We pack up and ride just long enough to find a bigger stream. Dad smells so bad that I get dizzy twice from holding my breath against the stink. We wash and dry what we can in the stream we find, and it's just nice to be away from where we were before. Dad sleeps again, but not the scary sleep. He's not so sick today, but weak, and he lies down every chance he gets.

When we get on the road, things look different than they did two days ago. There are a lot of cars that must have run out of gas and got left on the side of the road. I ask Dad about all the stuff on the road too, and he says that probably people tried to carry stuff after their cars ran out of gas, and then it got too heavy and they left it. I see a bag of groceries, so we stop and I run back and get it, which is good because we're almost out of food. It's pretty cool to look through someone else's groceries. Mom never lets me eat as much junk food as there is in the bag, but Dad just grunts.

People are walking on the road, and I can tell some are out there to look through stuff that got left behind, and others must have run out of gas.

It is good that we are on a motorcycle because some spots between cars are really narrow. Most people pulled over to the side as they ran out of gas, but some folks must have tried to get every last inch and their engines died right in the middle of the road.

We don't make very good time, and there's too much junk everywhere to drive at night. We stop in the middle of nowhere after we find more food. I find four big beers, too, and I dump them out quietly without telling Dad.


We eat potato chips for breakfast and wash them down with some Mountain Dew. It's not as great as I thought it would be. Plus, the Mountain Dew is warm. Not long after we get back on the road, we see a sign that says CHICAGO 108 MILES. The longer we ride, the more cars and people we see, so now we go slow enough that Dad and I can talk while we ride.

"Where are we, Dad?"

"We're getting close to Chicago, Bub." I know Chicago is a city, but I can't remember what state. Dad must feel me thinking so he shouts back, "We're about halfway to Vermont."

I think about this for a little while. I know we have used up five of the gas cans already and most of the food.

"Dad, can we buy gas here?"

"We'll see, bub."

"What about food?"

"We'll figure it out, all right? I'm thinking maybe we should avoid Chicago." Dad thinks for a minute. "Who knows what the cities are like right now."

We are quiet for a minute, trying to imagine, and then Dad says, "We'll get a boat."

"A boat?" I ask. "What for?"

"We could sail through the Great Lakes. You don't need gas for that." Even though I can't see his face, I can tell Dad is thinking out loud.

"We could fish, maybe," I say to be helpful.

Dad is thinking too hard to answer.

We get off of Interstate 90 and start heading north toward Milwaukee. Soon there are cars everywhere. Cars that are stopped and empty. Cars that are trying to wiggle through the other ones. Cars that look like they've been looted. Cars with whole families standing around them. There are people everywhere on the road, walking away from the city. Some parts of the road are like a zombie movie. Everybody is just shuffling along with a dead look in their eyes. Sometimes people reach out to Dad and me like the seaweed people in the *Little Mermaid* movie. We go slower and slower.

A little before lunchtime we get to a spot in the road where we can't get by all the abandoned cars because they take up the whole road. Dad stops the bike and stares at the trailer for a minute. An old Indian-looking guy offers to buy the motorcycle, but Dad just shakes his head. Dad unhitches the trailer and tugs it off to the side. A black woman offers to buy the trailer. Dad tells her it's hers if she wants it. A white teenager asks if the motorcycle is for sale, and an older guy says he'll double whatever the teenager is offering. I am getting nervous about sitting still. Everybody wants our bike.

93

Dad hands me our last gas can, climbs on the bike, and shoves the garbage bag of our stuff between his legs. I try not to make eye contact with all the people who are staring at us. A few of them call out to us, but Dad just waves and keeps going. I see a lady in a really fancy dress carrying her high heels and an empty bottle of champagne. I see a garden cart filled with books. There is a hamster cage on its side with two tan hamsters huddled inside.

I am more than a little nervous from all the people walking around on the highway and all the cars and stuff everywhere and every bit of it just feeling wrong. We don't stop for lunch, or for anything really, except twice when Dad has to move things out of the way. Everywhere I look, people are worried or exhausted or empty eyed. If I look up, there are fingers of smoke worming into the sky in every direction. After a while I just bury my head against Dad's back and try not to breathe too much gas fumes.

When we finally stop in the late afternoon, I have that feeling in my vision that we are still moving even though we aren't. Somehow my dad has found a big boat parking lot and there are boats everywhere. A *huge* lake, I mean so big I can't see the end of it, is in front of us.

We get off the bike and kick our legs out, and I put the gas can down next to the bike and walk away for fresh air, but Dad calls me back.

"Stay close," he says, and I notice how some groups of people are staring at us. Right away a black guy in clothes that were pretty fancy but are now wrinkled walks up and offers to trade us his watch for the motorcycle.

"It's a Piaget," he says.

"Not interested," says Dad.

Dad tells me to pick up the gas can. The guy offers me the watch for the gas.

"Not interested," says Dad. "Sorry." He pushes the bike up a little ramp out onto one of the docks. There are boats parked on both sides, some really big, some just normal. We walk past a big boat and see a group of people up on the deck. They are acting kind of crazy, dancing to music and waving drinks around.

"Hey, handsome, come to our End of the World Party!" shouts a dark-skinned lady with a red mouth. Dad gives her a nod and we keep going.

"What are we looking for?" I ask.

"A sailboat, I think," says Dad. "One small enough for the two of us to sail, but big enough for the bike." We walk to the end of the dock and Dad doesn't see anything that suits him, so we go to the next one. Some people carrying bags of stuff hurry down the dock and brush by us. I can tell they've been stealing. I am ashamed for them, and then I realize exactly what we're doing.

"Are we going to steal a boat, Dad?"

Dad clears his throat. "You could call it that, I guess," he says. "But I'd rather say 'liberate.'"

"Do you know *how* to liberate a boat?"

"Never liberated anything bigger than a canoe before," says Dad. "And we always gave 'em back."

I am a little relieved that Dad seems nervous about stealing.

"What about sailing?" I ask.

"I've always wanted to learn," says Dad, and he grins at me with one side of his mouth. I grin back. I really get into the spirit of things now. I point at a boat with big, fancy writing on the back.

"What about that one?"

Dad frowns and looks down his nose.

95

"Too much brass and navy. I was thinking of that one." He points to a sleek red motorboat that looks like something James Bond would drive.

"No sail, Dad."

"Darn," says Dad.

I point out a colossal boat that has four Jet Skis on the back, and Dad turns it down for not being roomy enough. We're really beginning to laugh when we hear some incredibly bad words coming from a sailboat down on the end of the dock. A short man storms out onto the deck, waving a wrench and continuing to cuss in a way that would have me grounded for a week. He gives one of the chairs a savage kick, but it doesn't budge because it's bolted down. The man howls and grabs his foot and then throws the wrench, badly, to where it tumbles to a halt in front of the motorcycle.

"Engine trouble?" asks Dad in a nice tone of voice.

The man says lots of bad words, but I understand that he's mostly wounded because *the one time* he's not working his *butt* off and can actually use the *darn* boat, it won't start! And the *so-and-sos* at the marina, who he's paid to do nothing for fifteen years, aren't around to help him the one time he *actually* needs them to do something. And his ex-wife stocked the boat with diet food he can't stand and rosé he can't stand and books he can't stand and art he can't stand and not one useful thing about how to sail a *gosh darn* boat.

"How much food do you have?" asks Dad.

"It's none of your #$%*ing business," says the man.

Dad shrugs and tosses the wrench back up onto the deck. It skids to a stop right at the man's toe and I'm more than a little proud of my dad.

The man glares at him and we keep walking, though I can feel the guy's eyes burning on the back of my neck. We haven't gone far when I hear him limping down the dock after us.

"Hey!"

Dad keeps walking, so I do too.

"Hey! Listen, buddy, you know how to fix an engine?"

Dad half turns and says, "Maybe I do. None of your business." Then we keep walking.

More swearing and the guy limps a little faster. "What do I have to do, beg? Okay, I'm begging. PLEASE help me fix my engine and I'll . . . I'll give you a case of rosé."

I wish I knew what he's talking about, but Dad keeps walking, so it can't be that good.

"And some food. Four meals of anything you want."

"How much food do you have?" asks Dad.

"Cases of it. It's all crap. Dried fruit, rice meals, low-cal everything, but the hold is packed. Party crap too. Nuts, olives, crackers . . ." The man talks so fast I can barely keep up with my ears.

"Fuel?" asks Dad.

"Diesel. Gallons of it. Tens of gallons, but I'm not offering the diesel. You know what it cost me two days ago? But I'm not offering."

"I'll take a look at your engine," says Dad. "Then we'll talk."

We back the bike up to the guy's boat and he complains about it a bit, but in the end he lets us park the bike on his deck. It's not easy getting it on the little walkway, but my dad is wicked strong. Then we're all on the boat, standing too close to one another because there's not too much room with the bike, and the guy looks up at my dad, who is at least a foot taller, and I can tell he's already regretting this, because there is a little

97

silence. Then Dad nods toward some narrow stairs. "Down there?" he asks.

The man nods. "Take a hard right at the bottom. There's tools and stuff—you'll see." The man sort of gives up then and collapses on a light-blue bench that lines the side of the boat. Dad ducks his head low, steps down some stairs and disappears below.

I look around. The boat is named *Need a Lift?* and is all done up in white and gold and pale blue. The place I'm standing is a deck at the back that has benches along both sides and a table down the middle. The motorcycle takes up most of the space in between the table and one of the benches, and in the back is a big pedestal with one of those big boat steering wheels attached to it, plus some screens and levers and buttons. Everything looks sleek and expensive. I realize I'm carrying the gas can and the garbage bag full of all of me and my dad's worldly goods. I try to put them down quietly, but I get the feeling this guy has already noticed that we're not exactly yacht people.

"What's your dad do?" the guys asks.

"Mechanic," I say.

"Right, kid. Mechanics don't look like that. He's an actor, right?"

"No, trust me. He's a mechanic."

The guy grunts. "Where are you going?" he asks.

"We're trying to get to Vermont. My aunt lives there—"

"Me? I'm trying to get to Nantucket." He interrupts like I wasn't even talking, and I can tell he's the kind of grown-up that doesn't know that kids have brains too. "I've got this beautiful place, right on the water. I've been there, like, six times in ten years, but I love it every time. Plus, Nantucket's out there, way off the coast. They'll leave it alone."

"Who will leave it alone?"

"Whoever did this!" The guy waves his hands at everything. "Terrorists! The government! That Cheeto in the White House! The people! I don't know, kid! I'm a surgeon. I pay my taxes. I work eighty hours a week making beautiful women more beautiful, and old women young, and fat people thin, and I expect other people to do their jobs while I'm doing mine. I don't know who did this. What have you heard? Occupy Wall Street, I heard, with the army. Sheesh." He glares at me like I asked him something rude.

Luckily, Dad comes up then.

"I can fix your engine," he says.

"Great! Do it! You can take whatever you want out of the kitchen—the galley—whatever."

"I appreciate that," says Dad. "But if you want me to fix your engine, I'll need something else."

The guy freezes and frowns up at Dad.

"We want a ride to the other end of this lake."

"You want a ride?" wheezes the man.

"Yep," says Dad. "We're going to Vermont, so we'd appreciate a ride as far east as you can get us."

"So you fix my engine in what, two, three hours, and then I give you a ride for three or four days? No way. NO way. NOT happening, buddy."

Dad shrugs and rubs his chin. "How long you think you can sit here with a hold full of rosé before they get tired of going after the empty boats?" Dad points to a guy three boats down who is piling stuff from the boat onto the dock. Another guy is standing over the stuff with a small black gun. "Or them?" Dad points over to the End of the World Party boat. "I think they're about two drinks away from lighting the dock on fire."

The man says some more bad words. "Fine," he sneers. "I control the hold, okay? Nobody gets food without my permission." He pauses for a split second. "We share the work. We sail as much as possible. I dictate direction, speed, everything. You fix the engine, this time and every other time it breaks for no extra charge. I get the master cabin."

I have to admit that the guy is a very quick thinker.

"We get three meals a day and water, and you let us out as far east as you can get in these lakes," says Dad.

"In the lakes, not the canals?"

"As close to Vermont as we can get."

"I'm Dr. David Pansky," says the man, holding out his hand.

"Jerry," says Dad, shaking hands.

Nobody says anything about me, so I stand up and say, a little too loud, "I'm Caleb."

Dad brings me down to a really tiny room that is jam-packed with shiny, brand-new engine stuff.

"Guy must be a real idiot," he says in a low voice. "Only thing wrong with this engine is that the battery's unplugged to keep it from draining." I snicker like I know what that means. "It'll take me three seconds to fix it, but I'm going to hang out here a little longer so he feels like he's getting his money's worth." I snicker again. "I want you to find out how much food and gas he has. We should trade that rosé for some more diesel or food from those morons on the party boat."

"What's rose-ay?"

"Wine. Can you carry a case of wine?"

"I guess."

"Go trade. Tell the doc we could use some coolant, but just get fuel or food or water first, okay?"

"Okay."

"If anyone bothers you, just jump in the water."

"'Kay."

"Bring me a book or something. It's going be dull down here."

I poke my head up to the deck, but Dr. Pansky's not there so I look around in one of the rooms under the deck. All the furniture looks like it's supposed to be aerodynamic and is the same colors as the outside of the boat. Dr. Pansky is in a nook that is crammed with controls, staring at some maps.

"What?" he says without looking up.

"Dad says we maybe need coolant and more fuel. He says we should trade the rosé wine to the party boat."

Dr. Pansky nods, frowning, then leaps into action. Soon we have thirty-two bottles of pink wine in a little wagon. Dr. David goes all oily and nice, and the people on the party boat happily trade us twenty gallons of diesel for the wine. We coulda got more, but we ran out of containers for the diesel. We go back to our boat, and then Dr. David says we should do some looting, too.

It turns out not to be very hard to break into a boat because the locks are really flimsy.

"That expensive alarm system isn't going to do much now," cackles Dr. David.

We do three boats and get a bunch of fancy pasta, some cases of water, and some dirty magazines. We stack everything in the wagon. I also find a solar battery charger, and I think that Dr. David actually likes me for a second. Lots of good stuff is screwed down, but we draw the line at actually breaking things. We're about to go back out with a screwdriver when Dad comes up, wiping his hands on the back of his jeans.

"Give 'er a go, Doc." He winks at me.

Dr. David goes to the pedestal with the steering wheel, where there's some controls, and does some stuff with switches and a key. Somewhere deep in the boat a low rumble starts and I hear water start to splash. Then I hear the music stop and some yelling. It's dusk now and hard to see, but the water carries the sound of an angry group of people.

"We need our diesel back!" somebody yells.

"Let's go," my dad yells.

Dr. David is grinning. "Cast off!" he yells. "Anchors aweigh!"

Dad leans over the edge of the boat and unwraps a rope from a big metal cleat. I see one farther down and work on it. The angry people sound closer. I get the rope free and Dad yells back to Dr. David. "Get going, they're coming this way!"

I can see a number of folks from the party boat walking unsteadily down the dock with some other very sober-looking people behind them. One of the party boat people points at us, and the sober men push them aside and start jogging down the dock.

"Go!" yells Dad.

Dr. David laughs like an evil villain in a movie and pushes a lever forward. There's a creaking sound and then two mighty cracks. Dad and I forgot the ropes on the other side of the boat. The cleats rip free from the dock and with a roar and shouting we're off.

# Chapter Fifteen: Mistake #1 Revisited

## Leah

While she was hiking, Leah could forget about everything for hours at a time. The trail was worn by thousands of footsteps, so that it felt like she was walking along the bottom of a dry riverbed, three feet below the forest around her. She invented things in her head, mechanical things. She invented a tent that popped open from its case ready to sleep in. She invented a wind-powered rotisserie for the camp stove, a water filter that worked by centrifugal force. She'd have just solved some design problem—such as slowing the rotisserie in windy weather (rattail screw)—and there would be Sam, waiting for her at an intersection or at a stream.

"We should get water here?" he'd say, and everything would come rushing back to Leah like a punch in the gut.

Other times she obsessed about how to get home. She had decided without realizing it that she'd walk home. She liked the idea of making it there without help from either of her parents, but Sam didn't have maps of anything but the trail. Leah couldn't picture how to get from the trail, which went through the middle of New Hampshire, back up to northeast Vermont. Sometimes she felt like if she squinted hard enough at the picture in her brain, she could see it like a real map, but that just made the miles leak by slower than ever.

Leah and Sam had exhausted small talk pretty much immediately. They both listened to music nobody else had ever heard of, including each other. A hatred of pop music will only take you so far in a conversation, and since Sam was going to be a sophomore and Leah had only done half of her junior year at Wiltmore, they couldn't really compare notes on teachers or classes. Leah knew that she wasn't going to offer up any stories from her sordid past, and it seemed like Sam was just as reluctant to air his dirty laundry.

Sam said everything as a question, so both nights he'd studied his map and then said, "We hiked 16 miles today? That's 31 miles so far?" Both nights they'd eaten something for dinner and then set up the tent. They avoided getting into the tent until the last minute, and they feigned sleep immediately. By the third night they'd run out of pasta and had to eat some of Ms. Goss's candy for dinner.

Leah sighed at the 73% cacao extra-dark chocolate bar she was holding.

"Isn't this every girl's dream?" said Sam. "To eat chocolate every meal?"

Leah raised an eyebrow. "Look at you. You're making a joke!"

Sam snorted.

"Actually, I think I'd do just about anything for a salad right now. Even one of those limp, warm salads from the salad bar," said Leah.

"Even with that orange dressing?"

"Thousand Island? I love that stuff!"

104

"Not me," said Sam. "I'll stick to chocolate. Or a burger. I'd walk barefoot all day tomorrow for a real burger at the end of the day."

"And fries. And a Coke. The kind from a bottle with the little drops forming on the side."

"And a pickle," said Sam, grinning.

"I'm not saying my mom doesn't drive me crazy, but she makes this drink, like a smoothie sort of, with watermelon and lime and mint and some other stuff all blended up. It's amazing." Leah paused and took a dubious bite of her chocolate. "So what are you going to do? I mean, you can come home with me if you want. My mom is major crazy, but my dad's okay sometimes."

Leah chewed some more. "My little brother's pretty cool, actually—wicked smart. You are the same age as my sister. You could fall in love with my sister." Leah wiggled her eyebrows and grinned at Sam.

Sam threw a piece of twig into the dirt. "You like your family? I mean, they're cool and stuff?"

"Yeah," said Leah. "I mean, except my mom. She's harmless, I guess, but totally plastic."

"Surgery?"

"No." Leah snorted. "We're not actually that rich. I am the rare Wiltmore scholarship kid. I just mean the things my mom cares about are so stupid." Leah thought a minute. "You know, after my . . . what I did—my accident—all she cared about was if the people in her book club would still talk to her. She didn't even let me talk to Janie's parents. She made me talk to a lawyer first."

"What happened?" asked Sam, wincing like he was afraid to know the answer.

"Oh." Leah frowned and sucked in a breath.

Most Wiltmore kids had perfected the art of revealing why they were at Wiltmore. Leah's delivery always earned some respect. She used a light tone and a blank face.

"I got drunk and killed my best friend."

Sam frowned and looked away. It hadn't gone over the way it usually did with other Wiltmore kids, who usually said, "Sucks," then countered with some tale of their own.

"I mean, not with a gun or anything. It was a car accident."

"You were driving?"

"Yup." Leah thought, or pretended to think. It was part of her delivery, a part most kids at Wiltmore could relate to. "Actually, I was so drunk, I honestly can't remember, but it was my car, so . . ." Leah shrugged and raised her eyebrows.

"So you crashed and then you both got out of the car?"

"No, we crashed and I got out of the car and she didn't— or she did but not soon enough—look, we don't know." Leah hunched over her knees and began to pick at the side of her shoe. "We were driving along this lake. It was a winding road and we flew off the road into the water. I don't remember much. Just sitting on a rock by the side of the lake, shivering, but not really feeling cold. I remember being pissed at her because she was taking so long and I wanted to get going. We were going to another party and my boyfriend—now my ex-boyfriend—was waiting for me. Then I started thinking that maybe she'd started walking without me, so I started walking down the road, and I kept walking until I could think straight and then I started running back, but it was too late."

Leah opened her eyes as wide as they'd go so that the tears wouldn't drip out. She never cried at Wiltmore. Never.

"Some guy picked me up. Called 911." Leah huffed out a half laugh, half cough. "It took all day to find the car because it went so far out into the water—really deep. They didn't find Janie until the next day because she wasn't in the car anymore."

They were quiet for a minute, then Leah got up and started folding up the chocolate wrapper. "Yeah, so it was jail, probably, or Wiltmore for me. My mom couldn't wait for me to stop being around town, embarrassing her."

"But you weren't hurt at all?"

"Nope. Just this weird scrape." Leah showed Sam a stripe of puckered skin that went from her right collarbone down toward her left breast. "I didn't even notice for two days."

Sam was quiet and Leah was pissed. It happened every time she thought about the whole thing. She was either so angry she felt like chewing up her own teeth or so sad she couldn't breathe. Angry was better. She tossed the chocolate onto a rock and turned away from Sam.

"Dammit." Leah walked up the trail a little ways and stared into the darkening sky, trying to catch the exact moment when she couldn't see color anymore. When it got too dark to see, she crept back to the tent and crawled inside. Sam was already lying down, taught and nervous. Leah lay down as quietly as possible and stared at the dark with her fists clenched at her sides.

She hadn't picked up her antidepressants before they shut the infirmary at Wiltmore. Leah couldn't tell if the weight she'd begun to feel was from that or from the whole situation she was in. She didn't care, really. She deserved everything she got.

# Chapter Sixteen: Last Drop of Ketchup

## Margot

Between being up at dawn with the smoker, and going to the antique stores and the recycling center and the library, by dinnertime I felt tired but saintly. Mom had run out of Diet Coke and was going through caffeine withdrawal. Also, she'd remembered that she hadn't filled her sleeping pill prescription, and the combination had been too much, so she'd stomped upstairs dramatically and slammed her door.

I was starving, a feeling I'd almost forgotten, since we used to have so much snack food around the house. I discovered that I couldn't think right when I was hungry, which was why I had munched down a handful of raw spaghetti before Grandma plopped down a plate of cold burger she'd cooked that morning in front of me and the last of the ketchup. We didn't talk much, because cold burger and warm ketchup is not the kind of meal you can eat while pretending nothing is wrong. We didn't talk about Dad or Leah, but the idea of them made a wall around any conversation.

After dinner I heated up water from the plastic jugs on the counter and did the dishes, using only one gallon. I stood in front of the sink and dipped my head in a second pot of warm water, then let it all drip back into the pot before I scrubbed my hair with shampoo. Getting the shampoo rinsed out was the real trial, but I was going to my first high school party and darned if I was going to show up with greasy hair.

I could admit how much time I spent trying on different clothes, but that would just be embarrassing. Finally I dragged Lucas into my room and held up two T-shirts.

"What one do you like better?" I asked.

"Doesn't matter, you know," said Lucas grumpily. "It's going to be dark."

I stood mute and then grinned at him. "It's going to be dark," I repeated. "You're brilliant, Luke!"

Luke snorted and left the room.

I pulled on a teal scoop-neck shirt that Judy had talked me into buying. I hadn't worn it once because I felt like my cleavage was a black hole of staring, but in the dark . . . I decided to give it a shot.

I checked my phone reflexively. When, I wondered, was I going to get over the habit? It seemed risky to just head off into the night without confirming that anyone would be there. What if I biked all the way to the highway and nobody else showed up? Or worse, what if just one person was there to witness how I'd shown up alone? I sat on my bed, suddenly unsure. If only Judy could text to say that she'd definitely, definitely be there.

I wandered downstairs. Grandma was all alone on the back porch using up the last of the daylight. I decided to stay home with her.

My clean hair began to dry into little ringlets around my face. I decided to go.

The house was full of heavy quiet, waiting for Dad and Leah. I decided, definitely, to go.

I got a surge of energy pushing off on my bike down the hill. Even though it was eight o'clock, it was still light out and that lovely temperature where the air feels like a gentle cushion around you. The wind rushing past my ears seemed like a whispered invitation. *This is real life*, I thought. *You did things today that will help keep you alive.* The heat of that thought spread across my back like sunlight.

As I pedaled through the sweet evening air, it began not to matter if there was a party at the other end. The breeze caressed my face and sent delicate fingers along my scalp. The loudest sounds were birdsong and the hum of my tires. I had a headlamp, a sweatshirt, and some water in my backpack, and I felt ready for anything. I approached the road that led up to Judy's house, and sure enough, there was Judy coasting down to meet me as if we had planned the exact timing.

"Hey!" I yelled.

Judy stopped right next to me and put down one leg to balance.

"Oh, thank God," she said. "I was so worried I'd be the only one there."

"Me too," I said. I showed her how I'd brought my phone, just in case. She giggled and dug in her back pocket. She'd brought her phone too.

"Come on," she said. "It feels magic tonight!"

When we got to the exit ramp, Madison Hanley was waiting with a group of four other girls. She actually smiled and waved at us, which was completely disorienting. Not only did everyone seem super friendly, but they all looked like they were about eleven years old because of the bikes. When we rode up, Ashley Branton, whose mother was a doctor, was listing off the ways people had died already.

". . . a whole family, plus some old people died from the fire in Saint J., plus there's been at least five people who got carbon monoxide poisoning from trying to cook inside their houses with camp stoves. Another guy got shocked when he tried to hook up something to a car battery, there's been, like, five suicides—"

"I heard that only, like, half of the families who put their grandparents in the nursing home came to get them, so now there's just three people taking care of all these old people and they're running out of food."

"Did you hear there was a lady who had to have a C-section with no anesthesia?"

"NOOO!" We all clutched our wombs sympathetically.

Madison Hanley looked around, then flipped her hair over her shoulders. "So, should we go?"

Feeling like an elementary school kid again, I remounted my bicycle and wobbled up the ramp behind the other girls. The sun was beginning to set, and the heat rising from the warm asphalt was pleasant. I realized suddenly how quiet it was. There was none of the ambient hum of traffic, no electric buzz from streetlights, no drone of jets overhead. I shivered once and pedaled harder to get up the southbound ramp.

First, I was startled by how big the highway was. Each lane is much larger than a car needs, which is not what it feels like when you are driving. At the top of the ramp was a small white car. It had been parked off to the side and one of the windows was broken. Madison stopped her bike by the window and peered inside.

"A lighter!" she said, reaching through the window.

My conscience sent a sudden drenching rain over the evening. We were stealing from people who had been so desperate they'd left their car behind and walked away down the highway.

"Any food?" shouted somebody.

Madison stuck her head into the car, then twisted around.

"No food, unless you want to dig it out of the cracks in the seat. This is disgusting!"

"Car!" yelled Ember.

We all scooted our bikes over to the side and watched a minivan drive by. There was a mattress strapped to the top, and the inside was completely packed. The woman driving was hunched forward over the steering wheel, looking grim.

I waved to her. *Good luck*, I thought.

We pedaled down the highway toward Saint Johnsbury. Ember found an unlocked car and shared the Tic Tacs she found inside. I took one and put it to my lips as tentatively as if it were drugs. I caught Judy's eye and she shrugged, then popped her Tic Tac into her mouth.

We lagged behind the others until we were alone.

"I didn't think there'd be looting," I whispered.

"No kidding. Do you wanna go home?"

I pedaled slowly. "It's so nice out."

"I know. The air feels like lotion."

A burst of laughter beckoned us on and we sped up a little.

The northbound lane was hidden behind a band of trees, and I could hear occasional traffic on that side.

"Do you think that things are better in Canada?" I asked.

"That's the word," said Judy. "A lot of people are headed that way, plus almost everyone is trying to get out of the cities."

"God, imagine."

"I know. My cousin lives in New York, and I keep thinking about her kitchen. When I went to visit her last summer, there was no food in there. Just, like, soy sauce and some takeout mustard packets."

"What happens to a subway when the power goes out?"

Judy grunted. "And all the people stuck in elevators."

We pedaled in silence for a while and became aware of the sound of music up ahead. In the dimming light I could see a crowd of high school kids. Someone had a huge boom box, like from the eighties, and was walking along with it on his shoulder. People were skipping and doing cheesy dance moves and singing along. "Just a small town girl livin' in a lonely world . . ."

Plodding along toward the back were some girls from our softball team, so Judy and I rode up to them and hopped off our bikes.

"Judy! Go-Go!" Sharon, our catcher, shouted, and waved us over.

"Hey, ladies!" Judy grinned and we stashed our bikes off the road, then gave everyone hugs.

"What have you guys been doing?" asked Judy. "I mean, crazy, right?"

"I know," said Jen. She was blond and lanky, with limbs that were never still. "I actually read a book today."

"That *is* crazy," I teased.

"Lucky you," groaned Sharon. "My mom started a committee to organize the neighborhoods into water districts. She made me make thirty posters. By hand."

We all grimaced sympathetically.

"Wow, we need your mom up where we are," said Judy, then she launched into the story of the guy with the gun and Madison's dad suggesting they sell the water.

"Jesus, people are nuts!" said Jen. "This whole thing is going to blow over, and then how are they going to show their faces?"

"My grandma doesn't think this is blowing over anytime soon," I said. "We're planting gardens, rationing our food. She's ready for the long haul."

"Really?" Jen frowned. "My dad says he's just going to treat it like a vacation. He's actually tackling the projects Mom has been bugging him about for years."

"Yeah, I mean, the government has got to be fixing this right now. We won't be the *first* ones to get electricity and everything, but as soon as the big urban centers are taken care of . . ." Irene, our shortstop, shrugged.

"I heard it was the government who did this," said Sharon.

"Not the government, I heard," said Ellie. "The army. The army shut everything down to stop income inequality."

"Income what?" Jen had taken off her hat and was spinning it in the air and catching it.

"Income inequality," repeated Ellie. "Like the rich just getting richer, everyone else getting poorer."

"Is that true?" Jen caught her hat and looked at me. I was usually the one to help Jen with her homework. She was convinced I was smart, so I took a stab.

"Well, there are definitely a lot of poor people in this area, and a lot of them go into the army."

"Yeah, like, half our school is on free or reduced lunch," said Judy. "There's tons of welfare families around here."

"Those people don't even want jobs," said Jen. "They just sit around in their pajamas smoking cigarettes and getting fatter."

I shrugged uncomfortably. "I don't know about that, but think about the middle class. Our parents grew up pretty comfortably with only one person in the family working. Moms could stay home and there was still enough money to buy a house and go on vacations. But now both parents have to work."

"No," said Sharon, "that's feminist stuff. Women *wanted* to work back then, but they weren't allowed to."

"Not every woman wants to work," said Ellie. "My mom wishes she could have stayed home with us. Plus, child care took, like, half her paycheck."

"Wait, wait, wait," said Jen. "You're saying that the army did this so poor people will have more money?"

"No," said Irene, "they want to change the laws that make it so easy for rich people to influence how the government works."

"You mean, like, bribing politicians?" asked Jen.

"No," I said.

"That's called lobbying," said Judy.

We were getting on shaky ground now. I frowned and thought a minute.

"It has to do with how corporations are allowed to spend as much money as they want to support the candidates they want," I said.

"So?" asked Jen.

"Before, each person could only give a certain amount of money. That way, no one person could influence an election too much." I took a breath. "Now that corporations are allowed to give as much money as they want, the people who own the corporations have a huge influence."

Jen nodded once, then tossed her hat into the air again. "I get it." She caught the hat. "But how does all this"—she waved at the darkness around us—"change anything?"

We all looked at Ellie. She shrugged. "It's just what I heard."

"Well," said Jen, "nothing is gonna stop us from having fun tonight!" She twisted around and pulled a two-liter bottle of Sprite out of her backpack.

"Warm soda?" laughed Sharon. "We're really livin' now!"

115

Darkness closed over the sky like a huge, slow-moving eyelid. We ambled along, passing the bottle of Sprite, belching, and laughing. The social order that had tipped off balance when Madison waved to me and Judy was now completely overturned. I saw a computer nerd talking to a bunch of Frisbee kids: "Actually, the electric grid is really vulnerable. The whole thing has to be totally balanced so that the amount of electricity that is going *in* the grid is going *out* at the same time. There's not a lot of storage capacity. . . ." Someone else was saying, "Wait, so the virus just cooked the insides of all our computers?" It was weird how without our phones we were all a little braver.

I looked over at Judy and grinned at her. I could just barely make out her teeth in the dark when she returned the grin.

I realized suddenly that the people in front had stopped walking, and then the music shut off. We got jammed up together like twigs caught in a stream. There were headlights on up ahead, and the light came back to us in sharp slivers, stabbing my eyes.

"He says we can't walk any farther," shouted a soccer player from up front.

An angry murmur stuttered through the crowd and we all pressed forward.

I heard a man's voice but couldn't make out the words, and then a noise cracked open the night like an ax splitting wood. There were screams and the crowd shattered backward.

"A gun!"

"Don't shoot! Don't shoot!"

"I'm warning you." I heard the man's voice clearly now, and he sounded calm and reasonable. "Me and my family are gonna take a look through these cars. You might be out just having fun, but I got kids to feed. You wanna go waste your time, do it somewhere else."

We shifted nervously, like a herd of sheep in a pen.

"Go on, all of you. There's other folks out here who won't be so nice. You run into them, they'll shoot you and take those batteries you're using up for no good reason. Git. I see you got young ladies with you too. Not safe. Now git."

I couldn't see the man who was talking because he was standing up on the running board of his truck behind the headlights, which were blinding all of us. He sounded calm, but I still couldn't shake the prickle on my back, the feeling that any second he might change his mind and start shooting.

"Judy!" I whispered.

"Go-Go?"

"Come on. Jen?"

"Yeah."

"Sharon? Ellie? Come over out of the headlights." I felt Irene grab my arm, and we turned away from the beams, blind and quiet. All of us stumbled through the tingling darkness until we heard a truck door slam and the truck engine come to life.

"Holy crap," Jen squeaked.

That was the signal for all of us to exhale and start jabbering. The whole crowd swelled with noise, and the next thing I knew, we were all running through the darkness. Everyone was whooping and screaming, but I didn't join in. I couldn't, not when all I could think of was Grandma saying women's rights would be the next thing to go, and the man warning us that it wasn't safe for young ladies to be out. What did he mean by that? Now that the lights were out, was civilization over?

## Chapter Seventeen: 984 Miles

### Caleb

Today has been exactly the way all those hunting and fishing and camping trips were supposed to be. First, we woke up right as the sun was coming up. We *had* to do the wake-at-dawn thing for hunting, fishing, and camping, but this morning it just felt right. Dad and I shared a big bed in a tiny room toward the back of the boat, and even though Dad snored, I slept better than I have since I left Park City.

I took a shower in this little glass booth, and boy, did that feel nice. I used some really flowery-smelling soap that made my skin feel slimy and smooth. Dad used the same soap, I guess, 'cause when he came out of the bathroom, he sniffed his armpit and said he hardly knew himself. Then he farted really loud and I sniffed a big sniff of fart and said, "Ahhh, that's the Dad I know," and then we both laughed so hard that Dad had tears streaming down his cheeks.

After breakfast we unpack some brand-new fishing stuff from the hold. I find this awesome spear, really sharp, with a barb at the end for stabbing big fish and pulling them up out of the water. Dad lets me hold it for a while, until I accidentally whack him on the side of the head with the back end of it. He gives me a fishing pole instead, and we all sit out on the back of the boat in the sun with some fancy fizzy drinks and our fishing stuff and we fish.

So Dad and Dr. P. start telling stories, including ones I'm not usually supposed to hear, and we laugh some more. It turns out that Dad and Dr. P. grew up not too far from each other in Connecticut. They even knew the same girl, Claire Wilder.

"God, she was beautiful," says Dr. P.

"And legs . . . ," says Dad.

"How'd you know her?"

"She went to my high school," says Dad.

"Her family went to the same temple as mine. I used to sit as close as I could and just stare at her neck. I asked her to prom but she said no." Dr. P. shrugs.

Dad laughs. "I asked her to prom too."

"What'd she say?"

"She said yes." Dad grins.

"Oh, man. Some guys have all the luck. It's people like you who keep me in business. You're born looking like you do—tall, broad shoulders, and all that. You don't know what it's like to be short, skinny, and covered in zits."

Dad shrugs. "I'm guessing you were born with a trust fund. That's nothing to sneeze at."

"Sure, sure, but beauty? Athletic talent? That stuff gives you all kinds of advantages. I think of myself as the great equalizer. I make everybody look like you. For a price. You know, I once gave a guy a scar on his chin? That's what he wanted, scar just like yours. . . ."

Right about then I catch my first fish.

I catch two more fish, and Dad catches a really big one, and Dr. P. catches three fish too. And darn if fishing isn't actually fun, with all the sun and the breeze and the fizzy drinks out on the boat.

Dr. P. says the fish are probably poisonous from the pollution in the lake, but we're going to eat them for survival.

Dad has to teach me and Dr. P. how to gut a fish. Dr. P. watches him once and then does the next three fish perfect, so fast I can't believe it. I can tell he's proud and happy, too. He says he's the fastest scalpel in the West, and I believe him.

We're feeling so good there on the boat. We all get another fancy drink with bubbles in it and a squirt of lemon so we don't get scurvy like real sailors did. Dr. P. says he drank all the booze on the boat the first three nights of the blackout, and I think that Dad is more relaxed with no booze. I'm relieved too. We eat two of the fish, and it's the first I ever had that wasn't tuna from a can. No one notices that I don't complain about it, but it's actually pretty good.

Dad and Dr. P. keep talking about how they should put a sail up. At first everyone's a little nervous because none of us know how to sail. But after the morning being so great, we decide to give it a try. Dad and Dr. P. argue about what rope to pull and stuff, but it's good arguing.

My dad calls him Doc, and Dr. P. likes it so much he tells me to call him Doc too, even though he doesn't really seem like a Doc. Doc looks a little bit wimpy standing next to my dad, but he doesn't mind anymore after gutting the fish. Finally Dad undoes some ropes and cleats, and Doc pushes a button on the helm, which is the pedestal with the steering wheel on it. I hear a little motor switch on, and the sail suddenly sprouts up and climbs all the way up the mast. Everything gets loud then. Lots of flapping noises and suddenly I notice the wind. The boat turns to face into the wind, and right as I begin to wonder how a sailboat works, Doc does something with the rudder and the boat tilts, the motorcycle tips over, and then we're flying over the water, just roaring along. I think that I actually whoop with excitement, and I'm embarrassed until I hear Dad and Doc do the same thing.

I've never felt so great. The boat is like how I imagine a racehorse would be like. I stand up on the edge and watch the water peel away from the side of the boat until I feel dizzy.

Doc shouts, "Coming about!" I turn to see what he means and I hear or feel or see a terrific *crack*, and then I don't know anymore.

Doc's face is about four inches from mine and I can see his lips moving, but whatever he says is coming from underwater and I can't understand it. Then he moves and a light behind his head stabs me in the eyes, and the pain is so bad I just want to take off my head and maybe I scream or groan. Plus, Doc is doing something to my forehead that makes my skin tug. I close my eyes and then open them again. I'm going to puke, so I scrabble up, but man, does my head hurt. I try holding still, hoping that will make my head stop throbbing. I stop moving and feel the weird tugging on my forehead and wait for Doc's language to be English again.

It turns out I got hit in the head with the boom. It takes a while for me to figure out that the boom is actually a part of the boat, not just a noise. I got knocked into the water, but Dad jumped in and saved me while Doc figured out how to stop and turn the boat around. Dad says it took a long time. Doc says Dad should shut up. Doc sewed up my head for me because the boom, the part that goes along the bottom of the sail, split the skin on my forehead. Doc points out that he could have used help with the sewing but Dad couldn't be in the same room without turning green. Dad says Doc should shut up.

I am glad that even me getting whacked by a boom and almost drowning hasn't wrecked the day.

Doc gives me a pill. It's a painkiller, and he tells me it's one of the last three he has, so don't expect any more after this one. Everything gets sort of soft and floaty, and then I am in the slick-looking bed and everything rolls about in an uncomfortable way and finally I am asleep.

The next morning I wake up with a bad headache and my forehead feels sort of tight. Doc gives me an aspirin, not the heavy-duty pain pill 'cause now he has only two left. He won't let me go out in the sun without a hat on because he says he doesn't want me to mess up his work and have a scar my whole life. He's mostly worried about his work, not my forehead. He says the work he did on my forehead would cost thousands of dollars in his clinic and that's because it takes real talent to sew somebody up so they won't even have a scar.

After breakfast I crawl up onto the front of the boat, the bow, where the boom isn't. The deck sort of curves away and it's slippery, but there is a small, short rail that goes around the edge that I hang on to. I watch everything with all my strength, but there isn't very much to see except lake water in every direction. It starts to hurt my head, and just as I'm about to go inside, I notice another boat.

The boat isn't moving and no one is up on deck. I have to say that my first thought is that maybe it's empty and might have some stuff we could use, but as we get near, a man comes out. He's oldish and behind him is a teenage girl. I can tell from the way he stands he's trying to protect her, but she looks tougher than him by a long shot. Also, she's holding a speargun, which, I notice with a sort of hiccup, is pointed straight at us.

I yell to Dad and Doc and they slow down our boat and drift toward the other one.

"You folks all right?" calls Dad. He hasn't noticed the speargun.

The girl lowers the speargun and calls, "You got a needle and thread?"

Dad starts to say sure, but Doc has noticed the gun. There is a bunch of arguing from everybody about whether to keep going or not. Doc and the man on the boat want us to keep going. Dad and the girl want us to stop and help. We agree to give them a needle and thread, and the girl agrees to put the speargun away.

It turns out that they've just been attacked by pirates. Not eye-patch, peg-leg pirates, but two guys in a blue Boston Whaler with a gun. The old man said that he and the girl ran out of gas, and he was up on the deck alone when the pirates came up and jumped aboard without asking. They had a gun and they tied him to the captain's chair on the deck, then put the gun down, luckily. They were going to steal a bunch of food and whatever else they could find, when the girl came out and shot a hole in their boat and then offered to shoot a hole in them. I think I'm a little in love with the girl. Or I would be if I weren't so scared of her.

But now they need to make a sail, 'cause of no gas, and they don't have a needle and thread. We give them a needle and thread, and they warn us to look out for a blue Boston Whaler.

Doc decides we should have a watch, even though Dad points out that whoever is steering the boat could just watch out for pirates. I say I don't mind watching, because I'm not really allowed to steer. Dad shows me how to shoot his gun again, and we decide to keep it right inside the hatch where we can grab it if we need to. Doc has a gun too. A super-fancy-looking silver thing that's too heavy for me to hold with one hand. He tucks it into the front of his pants, trying to look tough.

Dad says, "If that gun goes off, you're gonna castrate yourself."

Doc frowns and cusses under his breath, but he moves the gun to inside one of the seat pouches. After that, I go up to the front of the boat and keep watch until I get dizzy from watching the water go by. My head is still a little sore, and with the sun and the wind in my ears, I get tired. I go down to me and Dad's room and flip through a big book about yachts for about three minutes before I fall asleep.

We eat some more fish for dinner that night, and I think I am actually getting used to the taste. Doc and Dad seem like they have been best friends their whole lives now. Every word they say to each other is a joke or teasing, but they like it. I can tell. I do some dishes, since nobody else does them, and when I finish, I come up on deck.

"Lake Michigan is over nine hundred feet deep, Mr. Wyoming!" says Doc. "You really think that this boat has nine hundred feet of anchor line?"

"All I know is we can barely keep the boat going the right direction in the daytime with the two of us," says Dad.

"Hey!" I yell.

"The three of us, I mean," says Dad, grinning. "Plus, we have no idea where we are, since we just drifted all last night."

Doc says a lot of bad words, and I decide to show them just how useful I am, so I leave them arguing on the deck.

Inside, I find a big boat manual in a fancy binder, and I look up "anchors." The book also mentions sea anchors, which are something you drop overboard and they slow down the boat from moving by dragging through the water.

"We have three hundred feet of anchor line," I announce to Dad and Doc. "I think we should use the sea anchors."

That starts them both making fun of me, in a good way. Now I have a nickname too. Captain.

We find the sea anchors, and I figure out how to set them up while Dad and Doc lower the sail. We drop the sea anchors overboard, and sure enough, the boat stops drifting forward. I grin at Dad and he scrubs the top of my head. Dad says he'll take the first watch. And it's true, he really is going to take the first watch. It's just so cool.

# Chapter Eighteen: Miracle #1

## Leah

Leah decided she could never be anorexic. She wondered how Regan had done it. All Leah could think about was food, and in her mind it was beautiful. Glossy vegetables, charred steaks, the orange cheesy stuff that gets all over your fingers from Cheetos.

Leah noticed that Sam had stopped saying everything like a question, starting yesterday, when they ate their second-to-last chocolate bar. Leah thought it was because he was too tired to make his voice go up at the end, not because he was getting more confident.

Leah tripped over another root. Hunger was making her clumsy. It was making her crazy, too. The sunlight seemed too bright and there seemed to be a static noise to everything. Leah would have cried, but she didn't have the energy. She'd have liked to be angry, but that took energy too. So she walked, she tripped, she tried to put her sneakers in the spot that took the least energy. Eventually, even thinking was too much energy, so she just went.

Sam was waiting for her at an intersection like he always did, but when she got to him, he didn't rise and hurry on as usual.

"We could go this way and try to get to a town," he said, pointing down a trail with blue blazes, "or we could just keep going." Sam slumped against his pack so that he could look up at Leah.

Leah plopped down on a rock and scooted forward to rest the weight of her pack on the rock. "How much extra mileage is it to the town?"

Sam frowned at the book and read, "'Four and a half trail miles to a dirt road. Five miles of the dirt road until you get to a paved road leading into town.'"

"So probably nine and a half miles and then a hitchhike?" Sam nodded.

"We don't really have a choice, right? We need food."

Sam nodded again. Leah shrugged. "Well, lead on, Macduff."

Sam didn't move.

"What?" asked Leah.

Sam swallowed and stared straight up into the trees overhead.

"We'll come back, right?" he said.

Leah stared, willing her brain to figure out what he meant.

"We'll keep hiking?" he added.

"Yeah, man." Leah grinned a grin she wasn't feeling. "We're having fun, right?" She swatted Sam's knee. And he smiled weakly at her.

"Actually," he said, "I think this is nice."

Leah smiled. It was a small smile, but real. Sam was really beginning to grow on her. "Yeah, it's beautiful, really."

127

"I want to eat my boots, but I feel . . . peaceful." Sam smiled up at the trees and sighed happily.

"Peaceful's good," said Leah. "Eating your boots, not so good. Let's get some food."

While they walked, Leah spoke to Janie. In her head, of course. Leah imagined that maybe her own life was a sort of TV channel that Janie could watch whenever she wanted. When she talked to Janie, it was half prayer, half conversation.

*"Hey, Janie, listen, I don't know what kind of influence you have up there, but if you've got any strings to pull, we could really use some food.*

Janie came down and flopped on an imaginary cloud over Leah's head. *Food, huh?* She made a bag of Cool Ranch Doritos appear and popped one in her mouth.

*You're such a tease. You can eat whatever you want?* Leah asked.

*Yeah. I just think of it and then poof. But first you have to make yourself feel hungry. We don't feel that, you know, unless we want to.*

*Cool*, said Leah. *It's all I can think about right now. So, you know anyone high up?*

*Like in the Miracle Department?*

*There's a Miracle Department?*

*Yeah, but we weren't exactly saints, you and me.* Janie grinned. Leah could see her grin perfectly. One side of her mouth was higher than the other, and one eyebrow was raised. It filled her with hope and broke her heart at the same time.

*So, what do you do all day? You and the other not-exactly saints?*

Janie would play ultimate Frisbee all day if she could. It would be like that day last May. It was the first warm day of

128

spring, and they'd all slowly stripped off layer after layer of clothes until they were in T-shirts. Their noses running, cheeks flaming, they'd played until they couldn't see the Frisbee anymore.

*There's games whenever you want,* said Janie. *I'll see what I can do about the food, though.*

"Have fun," said Leah out loud. Janie faded like she always did before Leah could say "I'm sorry." Before Janie could say "I forgive you."

Sam saw them first. It was a pile of backpacks leaning up against a log at the trailhead. Leah and Sam walked up to them cautiously. Leah kicked one with her foot. There were a few pine needles on it and some spiderwebs. Leah guessed they'd been there at least a few days.

"Do you think . . . ?"

Leah dropped her pack and touched one of the abandoned packs. With an authority she did not feel, she opened it up and looked inside. The inside was too dark to see, so she tugged on the first thing she found. A rain jacket. A sleeping bag, and then there it was. A bag of Peanut M&M'S. Leah whooped and waved the bag in Sam's face. Her hands were shaking when she ripped it open and then her mouth was full and she was smiling and chewing and snorting with laughter and Sam was too. They were going to make it.

That night Leah ate something called Cranberry Chicken Ruby, and Sam ate beef stroganoff, from fancy dehydrated camping packets. The food from the packs would last them two weeks if they stretched it. They had two dozen of the premade dehydrated meals, a ton of gorp, and dried food and candy bars. Plus, they had rain gear now, more gas for the stove, and iodine in case their water filter failed. Their bellies full, they lingered outside after dark, chatting comfortably for the first time.

Leah described the inventions she'd made up in her head, and Sam gave her suggestions.

"How about a solar-powered shoulder massager?" he said.

Leah considered. "It'd be heavy, but you could put the massagey things in your Therm-a-Rest."

"Invent something to make our packs lighter. Like helium packs or something."

"Trained birds that fly over our heads, lifting up on the pack."

"Ooh, a donkey! We need a donkey!"

"Okay. I'll invent a donkey."

They both laughed and ate more M&M'S.

"Where do you live, anyway?" asked Leah. "Is your place close to the trail?"

"I'm not going home," said Sam, and he said it like he was slamming a door shut.

Leah shrugged. "Come home with me, then. I'm serious."

"Maybe." Sam studied her, then smiled. "At least we've got enough food to get that far."

Leah thanked Janie a hundred times a day, prayed to her really now. For the first time Leah thought they could make it to Vermont. Two meals and eighteen miles a day, Sam had said. They were going to make it.

# Chapter Nineteen: Good-Bye, Phone

### Margot

I woke up and listened to the sounds in the house. No Dad and no Leah, but Grandma was in the kitchen cooking up more burger on the gas stove. The smell of cooking meat reminded me that I had biked several miles last night and that I was starving again. In the kitchen I folded some burger into a slice of bread and wolfed it down, then went out to the smoker. At that point I was pretty good at coaxing fire out of the coals. The trick was to scrape off the top layer of ash and then find a good ember to work with.

When the fire was crackling, I took a moment to enjoy the feeling of satisfaction that always comes with starting a fire, then headed back up the hill.

After breakfast Grandma showed me where she wanted the new vegetable garden to go.

"Not the lawn!" Mom complained. "We just got it reseeded last summer."

"Do you have any better ideas?" said Grandma, hands on hips.

Mom waved irritably.

Grandma turned to me and Lucas. "Now, it's going to be a huge job to rip up all the sod."

Mom whimpered.

"I want you to be sure to shake as much dirt from the roots as you can. We need the dirt."

"'Kay," I said. Lucas nodded.

Lucas and I worked out a system where I used a shovel to cut the sod in chunks and turn it over. Lucas came along after me and beat at the clods of grass to knock the soil off. It was slow going. After an hour we'd cleared only a patch the size of our kitchen table, and I was leaning on the top of my shovel, working some kinks out of my lower back, when Judy rode up.

She was out of breath and crying. "We're leaving, Margot!" she wept. "I only have a minute." Judy looked at me and the garden we were digging. "This is just awful!"

I jabbed my shovel into the ground and went to hug Judy.

"Where are you going?"

"We're going up to our camp in Maine."

"Did you tell your parents about the guy last night?"

"No, of course not, but they heard about a gang of folks who are stealing people's food right out of their kitchens."

I swallowed that bit of information and nodded.

"Hey," I whispered. "It's all right. It will be over soon and you'll be back before we know it."

Judy sniffled, hugged me hard, and then giggled hysterically. "You stink, Margot."

I laughed and tears started leaking down my cheeks. "See? This is what you're missing." I gestured to the patch of dirt Lucas and I had made in the lawn. Lucas was pounding on a lump of sod dispiritedly.

Judy hiccuped.

I punched her in the arm. "Go on," I said, grinning. "The sooner you get out of here, the sooner you can come back."

Judy hugged me fiercely around the middle and then wiped her eyes.

"Love you, dork."

"Love you too," I said.

We walked slowly to the end of the driveway, and Judy remounted her bike.

"Wait!" I said.

Judy looked at me, tears streaming down her face. I couldn't think of what to say.

"Come back soon," I said.

Judy smiled a sideways smile and hugged me again.

"'Kay," she said.

"Okay." I nodded, then stood there waving until Judy had coasted out of sight.

Leah.

Dad.

Judy.

I turned back down the driveway, grabbed my shovel, and dug until all my old blisters had ripped open and blood was making the handle too slippery to hold.


Lucas and I ate more dry burger for lunch. He didn't talk to me at all, but I knew that was just his way of showing he was sorry about Judy. He's a sweet kid if you know how to understand him. He followed me up to my room and we read, me on the bed, him on the floor, for about half an hour before we heard Mom and Grandma come in the door. I was half asleep, the book facedown on my chest, when Lucas poked me hard in the side.

"A car," he said. He bounded over to the window and looked at the driveway below. "Dad's home!"

We raced each other downstairs and out the front door. I beat him to the end of the walk to the drive by a few steps and pulled up short, putting my hand out to stop Lucas from running farther. Dad was still sitting in the driver's seat, hands on the wheel, looking blindly ahead of him.

"Leah," I said. "He didn't get Leah."

Lucas pushed past my hand and stomped up to the door of the car. He hauled it open and looked over Dad's lap into the passenger seat. He opened the back door and leaned inside, as if Leah might have been stashed on the floor. He climbed in and peered over the seat into the way back. Lucas turned and sat down hard on the backseat, then started kicking the driver's seat. Dad got out slowly, turned, and leaned into the back.

Lucas is ten, not exactly a kid anymore, but Dad lifted him up and carried him into the house, pausing to peck me on the top of the head as he went by. I could hear Lucas's quiet sobbing as they went past.

It was morning again. I lay in bed cursing the birds who were going crazy outside. There must have been a hundred of them, all with different songs that they were singing at the top of their voices. The sky was that piercing blue that meant it would be hot in the sun and cool in the shade all day. In other words, it was a perfect Vermont summer's day. I closed my eyes, the worry about Leah and Judy and everything like a throbbing weight on my chest. *I'll get up when this is over*, I thought. *In a week or two. Maybe.* And then, like a ping from my phone: *The smoker.*

*The frickin' smoker is what's getting me out of bed these days*, I thought. I got dressed and stared blindly around my room. My phone, sullen and dumb, was still on my bedside table. I shoved it into my pocket stubbornly.

134

Outside I squinted into the brilliant morning sunshine and started down the hill to the smoker. Crouching, I brushed the ash off the embers, but before I fed the fire, I thought to check on the meat. Squatting awkwardly in front of the tree, I reached up and unhooked a piece . It was warm, brown, shriveled as a twig, and absolutely rock hard. I blew some ashes off of it and sniffed it. It smelled smoky, all right, but was it done? Was it edible? I set my twig of meat on a rock and fed the fire a little bit. When I had a good healthy flame, I scattered a few of the last hickory chips on top and trudged back up the hill with the meat.

In the kitchen I showed Grandma and Lucas the twig of meat. Lucas grabbed it and knocked it on the table like a drumstick.

"Hey!" I said, but I wasn't really sure the meat was worth protecting. I looked at Grandma. She gave me an encouraging smile.

"Well done," she said.

"Is it edible?" asked Lucas.

"Good question," I grumbled. "It better be."

"Hand it over," said Grandma.

She took the meat and brushed it off roughly with her fingers, then laid it on a cutting board. Grandma leaned hard on the knife and managed to chop off three tiny slivers. All three of us looked at one another, grimacing.

"Count of three," I said. "One, two, three." I popped it in my mouth and chewed. And chewed. And chewed.

"A little tough," said Lucas.

"Salty," I said.

"But not bad," Grandma said, then swallowed. "And I think it will keep for a long time."

Again I had to wrestle with the feeling that maybe we wouldn't really need to eat the meat I'd smoked. It was nothing

I'd ever have considered eating six days ago, but I was still proud.

Lucas and I brought a laundry basket down the hill and then carefully smothered the fire, instead of dousing it with water, so that no steam would undo the drying effects of the smoker. We stacked the meat like so many twigs into the laundry basket and carried it up to the house. We decided to hang it in the living room, since it had the highest ceiling and the meat would be out of the way. When we were done, it looked like a collection of bizarre wind chimes.

"Wow," said Lucas with feeling. "We're going to be like cavemen."

I couldn't disagree.

That afternoon I put on my backpack and rode my bike down to the village just to get away from the house and the blame that was shooting around like lasers from everybody's eyes. Nobody could look at Mom anymore. Dad couldn't forgive himself for not ignoring Mom and getting Leah on the first day. Grandma was worried, and that feeling hung like smog in the house along with sadness and helplessness. None of us could even breathe.

The village of Canton Hollow had changed in six days. For one thing, there were people hanging around everywhere. A woman was selling chicks and chickens by the library. A group of people sat in the shade on the town green, each with a sign listing their area of expertise, and they all wanted food. SEWING FOR FOOD, MANUAL LABOR FOR FOOD, CHOP FIREWOOD FOR FOOD. There were two men standing by the carcass of a deer hung in the shade. A small group of people shouted offers at them.

"I'll give you a box of shot for a haunch, Ricky."

"I know how to tan that hide, if you want."

It was intimate somehow, without the windshield of your car to hide behind. You had to wave at everybody, or nod if you needed both hands to ride your bike. No cars went by.

The biggest change was a giant solar panel on the lawn of the library. Next to it was a sign pointing into the library that said: FREE DRINKING WATER. A kid Lucas's age was outside the library loading four plastic jugs of water onto a little trailer behind his bike.

I rode slowly through town to the post office. The same old man from before was sitting outside, although he had made some improvements to his station. Now he had the sort of shade tent you see at farmers' markets over a stuffed recliner and a big card table. He saw me stop and heaved himself importantly out of his recliner.

"You want to add something to one of my lists?"

"Your lists?" I asked.

"You here to report any dead, missing, or found? You got a skill or a trade? You looking for someone with a skill or a trade? Job?" As he spoke, he pounded the table where each list was secured by a large stone.

"Is it all right if I take a look?" I asked, curious.

The man sniffed to show that he didn't have time for idle gawkers, and then collapsed back into his chair with a grunt.

"They need weeders. The Lecounts, with the farm on Kirby Road? They got a field of cow corn and they're offering six eggs for a day of weeding."

"Oh," I said politely. When what he had said registered, I looked up. "Six eggs? For a whole day of work?"

"There's folks who are that desperate," said the old man, satisfied to have gotten a reaction out of me.

I looked through the list marked "Confirmed Dead," though it felt like bad luck.

Patricia Holder, July 10, possible stroke or heart attack
John Wheeler, July 10, crushed by tree
Abby Nelson, July 11, sepsis from cut foot
Gurney Raslen, Harriet Raslen, July 11, suicides
Rebecca Fern, Thomas Fern, Corey Fern, July 11, house fire

I stopped reading with a sick feeling in my gut. The next list was entitled "Missing." I found "Leah Deford, female, 18, of Canton Hollow, VT" and touched my mom's handwriting gently with my finger.

Next was a notebook with a bunch of messages.

"That's going to Saint Johnsbury in a couple hours," said the old man. "It'll go to the post office, but no farther. Costs a dollar or trade."

I had the urge to reach out to someone. I could write, "Ronan, the meat is done," but I was struck by shyness and also hopelessness. Was this what it had felt like in the Pony Express days? As if prayer was more important than postage?

"Thanks," I said, then remounted my bike and coasted back through the village. The woman with the chickens caught my eye again. People were working in a field all day for six eggs, I thought.

I hopped off my bike again and walked it up to where the woman was sitting. She was about Mom's age, but she looked content to be sitting there knitting something in the sun.

"Hello there," she said.

"Hey," I said.

We both stared at the chickens together. They were strutting around importantly in a big wire dog cage.

"I just love watching them." The woman smiled. "They're like little dinosaurs stalking around like that."

"Could I get one?" I asked.

"I sell them in fours, because they like to be in flocks. They'd be nervous without company."

"Well, could I get four, then?"

"Sure." The woman put down her knitting and looked at me. I realized this was when I should make an offer.

"Uh, I don't really have any cash," I said.

"That's fine, honey, do you have something to trade?"

"I've got an iPhone," I said. "No charge in the battery, though." I pulled my phone out of my pocket. I hoped the woman wouldn't notice that it suddenly looked like a small hunk of useless metal. She took it from me and sniffed it. "It didn't get the virus? Not melted on the inside?"

"I don't think so."

The lady expertly removed the battery and sniffed the inside of the phone. "Nope, it's good." She looked at me over her glasses. "Okay, honey, but you know this trade is forever, right? You can't get it back if the lights come on tomorrow."

"That's okay."

She put the phone on top of a laptop that was in a pile of stuff next to her chair, and I looked away before I could change my mind. I felt kind of blank, writing down my passcode for the woman. I barely noticed the completely novel experience of stuffing two chickens and two chicks into my backpack and riding up the hill.

# Chapter Twenty: 814 Miles

### Caleb

The next day Dad and Doc are both a little gruffer and puffy looking from not sleeping as much because of the watch. Doc is in a raincoat because it started drizzling early in the morning, but there is no wind. Even though the sails are up, we are barely going fast enough to have a wake. Dad and I eat breakfast, which is fat-free granola bars and coffee and sugar-free hot cocoa for me. While we're getting ready, I realize all the stuff I don't have anymore. I don't have a raincoat, for one, and it reminds me that I have been wearing the same clothes for five or six days. When I pull up the hood on the raincoat Doc gives me, the stink of my clothes gets trapped right up by my nose and it does not smell good.

I tell Dad about the stink in my clothes, and he tells me that the next sunny day we'll do laundry. Then he yawns so big that I hear his jaw crack.

"I'll do the watch," I say, and I stand up as straight as I can to show I really mean it. Dad looks me in the eye and nods, very serious.

"All right, buddy. You take watch."

Dad starts down the stairs and then stops. "Shout if the wind picks up." Dad pauses again. "You leave the gun in the bench, all right?"

I sigh, 'cause I really wanted to hold the gun while I was on watch, but I just shrug like it's no big deal. I wait till Dad and Doc are both belowdecks, and then I go get the fishing spear.

I stand there with one hand on my spear and the other on the rudder. The rudder makes feeble movements under my hand, but we aren't really going anywhere. I don't mind admitting that I pretend for a little while.

You really can't see too far in the rain, but sound does weird things out on the water in the fog. One time I see a sailboat like ours, far away and sort of going in the same direction as us, but at the same time I hear voices from behind me. Another time I hear a bell and then water slapping the side of a boat, but I can't see anything.

I hear the engine of a motorboat, but I can't tell where the sound is coming from. I'm standing under a roofed-in part at the back of our boat, so I don't see the motorboat until it's pretty close, because it comes from the front. It's not a blue Whaler, but something about the way it's headed straight at us makes me nervous, so I call down to Dad.

I stand there with my fishing spear, watching as the boat zooms up to where I am standing. It is a small motorboat, loaded down with gas cans and some electrical equipment. One man is driving and one man is standing up in the back. Somehow I have time to notice that the man who is driving wears a Led Zeppelin T-shirt and has extremely hairy arms.

The head of the man who's standing shows over the top of the side rail of our boat as their boat bumps up against the outside. He grabs the railing and does a sort of hop, and then he's standing up on the edge of our boat, looking down at me and then behind me, which is how I know Dad has come up on deck. Dad grabs my fishing spear above where I am holding it, and for a second everything stops and becomes more solid than it already is. I can feel my dad behind me almost as if I *am* him. I can see the guy in front of me, how he balances with his weight in his knees.

The guy, who is in a red raincoat and flip-flops, raises his hand. For a second I think he is just showing us his hand, but then my eyes find the gun he's holding and everything draws itself down into the barrel of the gun.

My dad moves. He steps in front of me, I think, and pushes me backward, hard, cuffing the side of my head. Then comes a noise, a blast, followed by a high-pitched insect drone. I feel my dad jerk on the fishing spear and twist backward, and the guy is shouting but I can't hear over the insect drone. I just kind of feel the vibrations in my chest. My dad is still standing in front of me and I know the gun has gone off and maybe the bullet hit Dad, and there is this reptile part of my brain that tells me, *Kill the man with the gun.* I am trying to wrestle the spear from Dad, and then I think, heck, I'll just kill him with my own hands, and the insect drone is so loud I can barely hear my own thoughts, and then Doc is there and I can feel the way the air is being shaken by the noise of more shots, but I still can't hear. I have let go of the spear now and am moving forward with all my might, but moving so slowly that it is like I'm pushing through cookie dough. The man in the red raincoat jerks and I see the fishing spear has blossomed out of his shoulder and he's tilting backward, and the last I see of him is the end of the spear.

Then somehow I am inside. Doc is slouching back on the bench by the kitchen table, and Dad must be up on deck driving the boat with the motors on. The boat keeps tilting up and slamming down, so I realize we are moving fast. I can't figure out how it happened already, but I can see through the hatch that Dad is wearing a clean bandage around his thigh, and Doc is slouching with his shirt off and a bandage wrapped around his torso, right under his ribs. His skin is white, blue white, like skim milk, and he's telling me to get a piece of paper, God damn it.

"What?" I shout. The engine is very loud and I still don't trust my hearing.

"Tell your dad to turn off the freaking motor. We're not going to make it and he'll use up all the gas!" Doc's voice is weak, and when the boat jolts because of a wave, he winces and gasps in pain.

I go up to Dad and tug on his arm.

"Stop, Dad," I say. "You're hurting Doc."

Dad freezes for a moment and the energy that comes off his skin is terrible and hot. He punches the dashboard with the palm of his hand, then turns off the motor. He punches the dashboard again and spins around me, then climbs up to the front of the boat.

The silence rings in my ears and part of me wants to stay right where I am. Away from Dad and his anger, and away from Doc and his pain. I am shivering like it's cold, and it's hard to think straight, but I remember the paper, so I go back down to the kitchen, grab a little notebook and a handful of pens, then go back to Doc.

Doc looks up at me and nods. I think he's thanking me, maybe for turning off the engine, maybe for the paper.

"You get shot?" I ask. It's probably a dumb question, but as I said, my brain feels like it's a million miles away.

Doc grimaces. "My spleen."

"Is that bad?" I ask. Another dumb question.

"I'm bleeding to death inside my own body, kid."

"You can't . . . ?"

143

Doc shakes his head. "Nah. Your dad thinks if he drives like James Bond, we'll make it to a hospital." Doc chuckles, sort of like a cough. "Can you write, kid?"

I frown at him and he says, "Yeah. Of course you can. You're the Captain." He smiles a little half smile, and I smile back to show him I appreciate the nickname. Then my body does another huge shiver and I drop one of the pens.

"You're in shock, kid, okay? It's why you're cold, but I need you to help me here."

I nod and shiver again.

"Write this down, okay?" Doc waves at the notebook and leans back warily on the bench with his eyes closed. "Write it to my son, alright?"

"'Kay," I say.

"Benjamin. His name is Benjamin. Tell him I'm sorry that I gave him the iPad for his birthday when he already had one. And we should've gone to the basketball game like he asked."

*Dear Ben*, I write.

*Sorry about the iPad and basketball.*

"Tell him I'm sorry about . . ." Doc swallows. "I'm sorry for making fun of the camp he wanted to go to and also I'm sorry about . . ."

I add, *Sorry about the camp.*

Doc swats his hand at me.

"No, cross that out. Tell him about how I'm dying, but I'm not going to take a painkiller because another guy, who is not dying, needs them. . . . No!" Doc swats again and does another little laugh. "Just tell him . . ." He breathes out a big breath. "Tell him . . . when he was a baby, we used to stay up watching the Bulls together with the sound off. I'd hold him and bounce up and down with him to stop him crying—he cried all night, but it didn't bother me because I didn't sleep much anyway—and this

144

one night . . . this one night, every time the Bulls made a basket, I'd go, 'Yeah!' really quiet, and I'd look at him and he'd laugh. Every time. The Bulls won that game with a hundred and five points, so that night he laughed more than fifty times. Fifty times," whispers Doc.

I write: *When you were a baby, you laughed at the Bulls and I love you.*

Doc waves me over so he can see what I've written down, and he looks at it for a while and then nods. "That's fine, Captain," he says. "Thanks."

Dad comes down the steps, not angry anymore, but sad, and he looks at Doc. He gets a blanket from somewhere and tucks it around Doc and tries to give him other stuff, but Doc waves him away.

"I want a sea burial, Jer," says Doc. "But put some clothes on me, for Christ's sake."

Dad moves to get clothes.

"After I'm dead!" shouts Doc, waving at Dad. "It hurts too much right now."

Dad sits down next to Doc, scrunched up on the floor like a huge kid. Doc smiles a little about that and closes his eyes again.

"Thanks," says Dad in a really gruff voice. "Thanks for patching me up and my kid, too, and thanks for the ride."

"It's been a hell of a ride, huh, Jer?" says Doc.

"Too bad we're such lousy sailors," says Dad, laughing a little.

"You're lousy. I was getting the hang of it." Doc goes to punch Dad in the shoulder, but it is more of a little tap. "Your kid's a treasure, Jer, all right? A treasure."

Dad pats Doc's hand where it rests on his shoulder.

"You hook up with her?" Doc whispers. "Claire Wilder?"

"Kissed her," says Dad, "and maybe touched her boob a little bit."

"Maybe?"

"Hard to tell through that dress."

"Liar." Doc grins and closes his eyes for a second. "She talk about me?"

"Yeah," says Dad. "The whole time. I had to kiss her just to get her to shut up. 'That guy's gonna be the fastest scalpel in the West,' she said. 'Guts a fish perfect,' she said." Dad kind of trails off and looks up at Doc, then he starts telling a story about going to prom with Claire Wilder and how pretty she looked and how she talked about Doc the whole time. He adds tons of details and keeps talking for a really long time.

Then he stops talking, and that's how I know that Doc is dead.

Dad brushes his hand down over Doc's face really gently to close Doc's eyes. He puts his fingers under Doc's chin and pushes up, because Doc's mouth is hanging open a little bit and we both know he'd hate it if he looked stupid like that. The horrible part is that it won't stay closed. Dad reaches under Doc really carefully and grunts, then lifts him up and carries him to his bed. Doc's arms swing in a gruesome way, like a corpse, and I realize that a corpse is what he *is*, and my dad is touching him. Dad puts him on the bed, places his arms at his sides, and pushes his chin up again. Now he looks like Doc again, except he has no shirt on and there's blood on his pants.

"Clothes," I croak. My voice sounds like I haven't spoken in fifty years.

Dad nods.

We have never been in Doc's room before, and the two curving walls are covered with identical panels. I open all the panels and discover that some are shelves and one is the door to

146

a bathroom, and finally I find one that is a closet door. Inside everything is very neat. The shirts are hanging in a sort of rainbow of colors, and each pair of shoes, even the flip-flops, has its own cubby. I look at Dad and he shrugs.

"Something with a collar," he says.

I pick out a blue shirt with a collar and buttons and a pair of white pants, then bring them over to the bed. I go back and pick out a tie that has sharks on it and the fanciest-looking shoes, which are shiny brown. There are socks in a drawer nestled like eggs in a carton. They all seem equally clean, so I pick out some white ones.

Dad puts on the shirt over the bandages and then takes off Doc's pants. Doc's legs are really white and hairy. The blood soaked through to his underwear. I look at Dad. He nods. I get some clean boxers out of the drawer.

When we are done, Doc looks pretty good. Dad pats Doc's shoulder and I pat his knee.

"Should I get his watch for his kid?" I ask.

"Good idea, buddy."

I nod and then pick up Doc's hand with the watch. His skin feels like the cheese on cold pizza. I think that I will never again eat cold melted cheese. Dad and I act like we know exactly what we are doing when we fold the blanket over Doc's body and face, then the other side and then up over his shoes. I take his feet, Dad takes his shoulders, and we heave him through the kitchen up onto the deck. We put Doc down on one of the benches and stand back a few steps.

I blink for a while, looking around. It seems totally impossible that it is still daytime, still the same day that we started with this morning. Dad is squinting around and I know he's thinking the same thing. He clears his throat and puts his hand on his heart.

147

"Dear God, please take care of Doc here, I mean, David Pansky."

The rain has stopped but there is a layer of dark-gray clouds hanging low, like a shield. The bottom edge of the sun drops suddenly below the shield of clouds, and for a second I am blind, but then everything is spangled and glinting.

"He loved his son and the Bulls and Claire Wilder," I say. "Also, he could gut a fish faster than anybody and he did a really good job on my stitches."

"He was a good guy to go fishing with," adds my dad. "And he was really getting the hang of sailing."

We are quiet then, squinting into the light that is like thousands of shards of glass, rocking gently on the deck, hearing only the water sounds of the boat. Dad looks at me, but I just stare at him to show that I don't know what to do next, so Dad nods and bends down to get under Doc's shoulders again. I grab Doc's feet and we do our best to slide him into the water with some dignity. I step back from the edge as soon as I let go and grab Dad back with me too. It feels like death is a huge hand that could reach up from the water and grab us, too.

"Bye, Doc," says Dad.

"Bye, Doc," I say. Then I wrap my arms around Dad's waist and hang on like I'm the only thing that is keeping him there on the deck with me.

"I love you, bub," says Dad.

I can't talk, so I just squeeze him harder. When I let go, Dad kisses me on the top of the head. We set out the sea anchors and sit on the deck without talking or moving. When it gets dark, we go in, and I fall asleep with my dad wrapped around me like a shell, like I am a turtle and he is the part that keeps me safe.

# Chapter Twenty-One: Miracle #2

### Leah

Leah popped a peanut into her mouth and felt the water on her tongue rush to meet the salt. She flipped the peanut back between her molars and there was that *crunch* and then an oily release of flavor. Would she eat like this for the rest of her life?

"We're in New Hampshire now," said Sam, tilting his head back to pour a handful of gorp into his mouth.

Leah looked around. She knew borders were arbitrary, but it did seem different. The mountains were more dramatic here, steep and rocky, and the trails were worn deeply into the soil. Now that she was well fed, Leah could take pleasure in hiking. Despite a very heavy pack, she was beginning to enjoy the scenery and the rhythm of their days.

In late afternoon they got to a hut in the middle of the woods. It was called Carter Notch Hut, according to Sam, and people could rent bunks in it. There were huts speckled along the trail from here to the other side of the Pemigewasset Wilderness, guest huts that were run by crews of college students. Carter Hut seemed deserted.

The main part was old, dark, and wooden, with a big, professional-looking cookstove inside and a woodstove for heat. There was a sink with running water, too, which made Leah grin.

Outside were some other small bunkhouses with mattresses and rough wool blankets and, *good Lord*, pillows. The final treat was an honest-to-goodness toilet and toilet paper. Leah and Sam explored everything, shouting to each other and exclaiming. Sam spotted a small pond not far off, and they both stripped down to their underwear and took a freezing-cold bath.

"Should we stay here tonight?" asked Leah hopefully. "We could do some laundry. I saw some drying racks inside."

Sam grinned and jumped off a rock with a whoop. Leah scooped a handful of water at him. "You want to stay or what?"

"Yeah, let's stay. This place is awesome." Sam climbed out of the water and stood shivering on a rock. He was short and thin, but his muscles had a nice shape to them, and he didn't act like someone was about to hit him as much anymore. He turned to grin at Leah again, and Leah realized that his grin wasn't so rare as it used to be.

"I'll get more soap. I'm washing my socks even if it kills every fish in this pond," said Leah, hobbling barefoot back to the hut.

"Wash mine, too!" called Sam.

Leah gave him the finger over her shoulder and then laughed out loud. It was a good day.

That night Leah and Sam cooked their dinner in the luxury of the kitchen and then washed it down with some hot cocoa they found in a cupboard. They found tea, too, and Leah was humbly excited to wake up and have caffeine for the first time since they'd left school. They washed their dishes, and Leah discovered that there was actually running hot water too. She filled up the sink and washed everything she could think of. It just felt so good to plunge her arms into the hot suds.

After dinner Leah and Sam sipped more hot cocoa out by the pond and swatted mosquitos. "You think all of the huts will be like this?" asked Leah.

"That would be amazing, huh?" mused Sam. "It should take about four or five days to get through the Whites but I kinda like it here."

Leah nodded. "Food though."

Sam sighed. "Yeah."

They picked up their mugs and tiptoed over the rocks back to the bunkhouses. Leah had put her stuff in one bunkhouse and Sam had put his in the one next door. She could hear him knocking around after she had zipped herself into her sleeping bag. Even though she was more comfortable than she had been in recent memory, Leah couldn't sleep. Finally, after turning over for the fifth time, she slithered out of her bag, gathered up her pillow, and left her bunkhouse. It was pitch black outside, so Leah shuffled along slowly. As she reached out to find the door to Sam's bunkhouse, she heard the door creak open and sensed someone standing there.

"Sam?"

"Hey."

"I'm sleeping in here."

"Oh good." Sam laughed. "I was just coming to sleep in your house."

After that, Leah slept like a child.

The next morning the tea was just as good as Leah had imagined it would be. Reluctantly they packed up their packs and decided to skip part of the Appalachian Trail in favor of a route that led more directly to the next hut. It meant they had to hike on the road, and for some reason the road made them both nervous. Two cars passed the whole time, one loaded down with what looked like the contents of someone's entire house.

They felt relieved to be back in the woods, the relief lasting until the trail reared straight up a mountain and Leah's mind went entirely to her leg muscles. After an hour she almost bumped right into Sam, who'd stopped atop a big boulder on the steep trail.

"Leah," he said.

Leah climbed up the rock with a grunt and then turned around. The view was stunning, and it filled Leah's heart with a beautiful sort of sadness. She gave Sam a high five and they stood there for another minute not talking.

*If this is it,* thought Leah, *if I die right now, it would be okay.*

They continued up the steep trail into some scrubby pine trees, and then even those petered out and there was mostly moss-covered rocks and low bushes, which seemed to have grown sideways. Finally the trail leveled out and they were walking over the spine of the mountain range. Up to their left was a summit that was bare and rocky. Down below Leah saw a hut.

"You think that's the next hut in the system?" asked Leah.

"Think so. Is anybody there?"

"Can't tell," said Leah.

She kept her eyes on her feet for the next ten minutes.

"Hey," said Sam. Leah stopped and looked down the trail. A person had come out in front of the hut, spotted them, and started hiking up the trail toward them alarmingly fast.

Sam paused and Leah stepped up next to him to watch the person who was leaping up the trail toward them.

"Friendly?" asked Sam.

"I don't think so."

Sam grunted and puffed out his chest a bit.

"Maybe I should talk," said Leah. "I'm a better liar."

Sam nodded but didn't deflate his chest. Leah almost hugged him, but she knew it would ruin the new toughness Sam was trying to project.

In a minute they could see that it was a boy, college aged, who was coming toward them. He had sandy hair and red cheeks. Leah took a few steps down the trail and then stopped when the boy did just a few yards from them. He wasn't even out of breath from sprinting up the trail, but Leah thought he looked a little softer and chubbier than she had expected.

"You can't stay here," he called more loudly than was necessary.

"We're hiking south on the trail," said Leah. "We don't need to stay here."

"Well, you can't come in the hut," said the boy gruffly.

The boy kept changing his arm position—hands on hips, arms crossed. Leah had the feeling that he was trying to act more unfriendly than he felt.

Leah shrugged, disappointed, but said, "That's fine."

The boy nodded and frowned at her. "Okay then." He huffed out a big breath and turned down the trail. Leah followed him, trying to keep up, but the boy hopped lightly from rock to rock, whereas Leah had to pick her steps carefully.

"You need water?" asked the boy. His tone was much friendlier now. He seemed to think that he had satisfied his duties of scaring them away.

"Yeah," said Leah. "We do."

"You should fill up right here, then," said the boy cheerfully. "Our pump is broken in the hut and we've been having to haul our water and boil it. What do you have, iodine? Water filter?" The boy hopped three more times and then turned

153

to smile up at Leah. He'd stopped by a small trickle of water. Leah guessed they were supposed to get water there.

"Water filter," said Leah. She wondered for a minute if he was planning to steal their filter or something, but then he started chatting about the broken water pump in the hut and Leah had a sense that he didn't have a mean bone in his body. Even so, when she took off her pack she was careful not to show him all her food.

"Pump broke a few days ago and no one knows a thing about how to fix it. Of course the construction crew isn't coming up here anymore what with everything going on, so yeah." He shrugged happily as if it were all a great adventure.

Leah grunted noncommittally and set up her water pump.

"You guys don't have an extra pump, do you?" Without waiting for an answer the boy chattered on. "Really the water's probably fine but we're going to run out of gas eventually. Bear wants to save gas in case we're up here all winter, but honestly, I can't imagine that this whole blackout thing lasts that long, right?"

Sam spoke for the first time. "Leah can fix your pump."

Leah stared at Sam, scowling.

"No," she said.

"C'mon. Everybody at school knows you're some kind of mechanical genius."

"Really?" asked the boy. "The pump's connected to the wind generator so—"

"She can fix it," said Sam. "I bet she can. Really."

"Oh, no way!" The boy grinned like the pump was already fixed. "That'd be great! We've been too scared to really—"

"I'll look at it," said Leah, "but I can't promise anything."

"Well, that'd be awesome. I'm Chunk, by the way. You're Leah, and you?"

154

"Sam," said Sam. "Nice to meet you."

Chunk chatted the rest of the way to the hut, and they learned that the hut system had closed down, but a few members of the crews had decided to spend the rest of the summer in the huts and none of the administration had even known enough about the plan to object.

When they reached the hut, Chunk stopped midsentence and stared at them as if surprised that they were there. Leah guessed that he had just remembered that he was supposed to have scared them off.

"Well, you can fix the pump, right?" He said this to himself more than to Leah.

Inside, the hut was golden and warm, all yellow pine and some sun-filled windows. Leah had the immediate desire to stay there the rest of the summer. There was the mouthwatering scent of baking bread coming from the kitchen, which made Leah's knees feel weak. Two college-aged girls were sitting at one of the large pine-board dining room tables, rubbing something into their hiking boots, and they glanced up when Chunk came in.

"Told you," sighed the dark-haired girl to the tall one. "Nice job, Chunk."

"You really sent them packin'!" said the tall girl in a garbled Southern accent. "Did he offer you lunch yet?" she asked Sam and Leah in her real voice, which was British, Leah thought.

Chunk flushed and scrubbed his hand through his hair. "Actually, ladies, I just found someone who can fix our water problem." He nodded encouragingly at Leah. Leah stared at him. She didn't know what he wanted her to say. For an uncomfortable moment it was silent, and then Sam piped up.

"We weren't going to come here. We were really scared of him. Honest. I've never seen anyone hike so fast."

155

Chunk grinned at Sam and slapped him on the back with a guffaw. "See? Just for that, I will let you have a slice of my wild-foraged sourdough focaccia bread." Chunk held his hands up like a snooty French maître d' when he said this, and leaped into the kitchen.

"CHUNK!" a voice thundered from a room that was out of sight. "NO FEEDING PEOPLE! WE TALKED ABOUT THIS!"

"YOU DON'T EVEN KNOW WHO THEY ARE!" shouted Chunk, moving about the kitchen. "THEY'RE GOING TO FIX OUR WATER PUMP!"

A short, compact boy bounded into the kitchen, vaulted easily over the counter, and came to a halt in front of Leah. Leah had the impression that a much bigger person had been squashed down into this guy, who was only about her height.

"What are you? Engineer student? MIT? What?" He thrust his chin at Leah and then at Sam, unsure whom he was supposed to be addressing. He wasn't rude, exactly. It was just that his energy left no room for small talk.

"No," said Leah. "I just—"

"She's a genius," asserted Sam helpfully.

"Another genius? We're up to our ears in geniuses, for all the good it does us. Please don't tell me that you're another Ivy League princess."

The dark-haired girl looked up from the table and hurled a rag at the boy. It missed him and sailed into the kitchen. The boy just swatted over his shoulder. The tall girl chucked her boot at him and hit him in the butt. The girls high-fived over the table, grinning.

The boy half turned to protect himself from more flying objects, but kept teasing the girls. "Harvard. Both of them, and they can't even fix a water pump."

The tall girl drew herself up in her seat and stared down her prodigious nose at the boy. "If it were a two hundred BC Etruscan pump, I assure you, I could have it fixed in a jiffy." Her voice was deep and rich, with a hoity-toity-sounding British accent. "Alas, being fluent in three dead languages does not help when it comes to modern plumbing. That's why we have you, peasant."

The boy shrugged and offered his hand to Leah.

"Scoggin," he said. "Peasant and ignoramus." It took Leah a second to realize that Scoggin was his name.

"Leah," she said, and then, because she liked these people already, she added, "Genius, hopefully." Everyone laughed.

Sam shook Scoggin's hand and introduced himself. The two girls unfolded themselves from the benches at the table and came over. The dark-haired one was distressingly lovely and shaped like a lady in an old-fashioned beer advertisement. "I'm Rainy and this is Screech." Screech was even taller than she had looked sitting down. She had narrow, slumped shoulders, beige hair, and almost no chin at all. She was saved from true ugliness by her eyes, which were blue and sparkling with vitality.

Leah shook hands all around and then heard someone else come into the dining room. She turned and saw a huge college-aged boy. He was almost twice the size of Scoggin and he moved sleepily.

"I'm Bear," he said, and Leah thought, *Of course he is.*

"Now," commanded Chunk. "Clear off that table and everybody sit down. Scoggin, could you set for seven? No spoons." Immediately the hut crew scattered and swirled like leaves in a wind. When they settled, the table had magically been cleared and set, and Chunk was bustling into the room holding a tray high over his head. He motioned for Leah and Sam to sit and then stood at the head of the table with a butcher knife.

157

Little wisps of steam wavered up from a cookie sheet that was covered with flat, golden bread. The bread was shiny and speckled with some kind of fragrant plant. Generous slices of garlic filled the air with a pungent smell. Delicate curls of cheese were scattered about the crust, and Leah found herself having to swallow the saliva that had collected in her mouth.

"Today we are dining on a sourdough focaccia made from wild-harvested yeast. I sprinkled the dough with an assortment of wild greens—"

"Is this safe?" Scoggin sniffed.

Chunk glared at Scoggin and continued. "Wild greens, and I marinated garlic with my own special blend of olive oil, butter, and herbs. It is finished with aged cheddar cheese." Chunk bowed and everybody clapped. He set about cutting the focaccia into elegant slices and arranging them in a fan on each plate.

"Chunk, I'm starving! Do you have to?" Rainy groaned, and indicated the fussy little motions that Chunk was making over the plate.

"The eye appeal is half the meal," said Chunk, not looking up. Leah had the feeling he said this often, but she was inclined to side with Rainy. It was torture waiting for everyone to be served. When they could finally eat, it was silent for a few minutes but for the sound of crunching.

"Ah, Chunk," said Screech, "you have, once again, exceeded my expectations."

Chunk nodded modestly. "I wish we had a good Parmesan." He chewed and closed his eyes. "What I wouldn't give for a *nice* olive oil. With this dish I would do a walnut oil, actually, to bring out the nuttiness in the greens and then Parm, in ribbons."

"Stop it, Chunk," growled Bear. "You're making me hungry again."

Chunk sighed.

Sam cleared his throat and sat back a little from the table. "How do you get the bread to taste like that? You said something about wild yeast?"

Chunk rubbed his hands together and began to speak animatedly about capturing yeast. Everybody else pushed back from the table and began clearing.

Leah followed Rainy into the kitchen with her plate and cup. "He's going to be sorry he asked that," said Rainy with a grin, nodding at Chunk, who was now gesticulating inches from Sam's nose.

Leah shrugged and put her plate down. "Serves him right," she said. "He thinks that I can fix the pump, but I don't really know that much about plumbing."

Rainy waved away the apology that was lurking in Leah's words. "Come on, I'll show you the pump and you can at least give it a shot."

The hut's systems ran mostly on a combination of wind, solar, and water power. The stove, the lights, and the fridges ran on gas, and Leah saw that there was a wooden platform out behind the hut filled with large gas canisters. She wondered how long the gas would last if she couldn't fix the pump and they had to keep boiling all their drinking water. Leah spent the afternoon under the hut, carefully taking apart the pump, greasing the parts, and putting them back together. She tried running the water in the sink, but nothing came out. She crawled back under the hut to the pump and stared at it. She was pretty sure that there was nothing wrong with the pump, so she found the power source and started following it back to the big batteries that collected the power from the solar panels. She found a mass of wires but noticed that the power was still live. She had just figured out how to shut down the power so that she could work safely when Chunk called her for dinner.

It was another masterpiece. Chili and corn bread, but so perfectly spiced that Leah felt like she was tasting chili for the first time. She was surprised to learn that Sam had made the corn bread. Leah told everybody that she hadn't found anything wrong with the pump, but that she was looking into the power source.

Scoggin frowned. "But the radio still works," he said.

"What else uses electricity?" asked Leah. Scoggin leaped up and off they went on a tour of the hut electrical system. Scoggin watched as Leah set about figuring out which wires went where, and asked her a hundred questions. Leah tried to explain to him why she thought what she did, because she was guessing. She found it was helpful to talk through her thoughts, and Scoggin, for all his bluster about Ivy League schools, turned out to be very bright. By the time dark came, they had eliminated potential problems down to one wire, and they just had to follow it through the hut to find out where along the line something had gone wrong. Scoggin and Leah got flashlights, and Leah was surprised to find that she felt so eager to solve the problem. Anticipation was an emotion that had been absent from Leah's life ever since Janie died. Leah felt almost embarrassed by it, but here she was crawling through the attic of a hut, shouting to Scoggin and giving him a high five when she finally found a dead mouse and a spot where the wire had been chewed.

# Chapter Twenty-Two: Eggs Again

## Margot

Lucas, Mom, and I were in the garden, getting ready to plant beans according to Grandma's strict instructions. My chickens were there too, and they helped by scratching at the soil, eating bugs and weeds. The lady was right. I loved the way the chickens looked so confidant and alert. The two grown chickens had each laid one egg a day, which was not a lot for five people, but somehow seemed a miracle.

Dad was doing his best to figure out the well pump, but it made us miss Leah. I think we were all thinking that she could have figured it out in half an hour.

We were just marking out rows when Ronan coasted down the driveway.

I stood up and tugged nervously at the bottom of my T-shirt.

"Hey," I said.

"Hey, Margot," said Ronan.

I smiled at him, thinking how I hadn't needed to send him a message after all.

"Meat's done," I said.

"No way! How'd it turn out?"

I shrugged. "I'll show you."

"Wait, I got something for your family. Mrs. Deford?" he called. "I brought you something."

Everybody stood up and walked over to us in the driveway. Ronan carefully removed a long, towel-wrapped package from his backpack.

"Do you guys have a gun?" he asked.

"Cool," said Lucas.

"No," said Dad. "We don't have a gun." The way he said made it sound like he wanted to give Ronan his lecture about gun violence, but Grandma had perked up, so Dad bit his tongue.

"Well, this is yours, then, if you want it." Ronan unwrapped the towel from around a long rifle and held it across both hands. "It used to be mine. It's a good beginner's gun, and I just cleaned it this morning. I've got ammo, too." Ronan looked up hopefully at us.

"Great," said Grandma.

"Now wait a minute, we don't really need a gun in the house," said Dad, unable to contain himself anymore.

Ronan looked seriously into my dad's face. "You can hunt with this," he said. "People are already—hunting, that is. Even though it's not the season."

"I'm just not—"

"People are getting desperate, Mr. Deford," said Ronan. "They're stealing food, and most folks up here, well, they've got a gun."

"None of us know how to shoot," I said.

"I'll teach you," said Ronan, smiling like himself for the first time.

"Good," said Mom. She gave me a mortifying giggle. "You teach Margot."

"And me!" said Lucas.

"No!" said Mom and Dad.

162

"Let me teach Lucas about gun safety," said Ronan.

"It's a good idea," said Grandma. "If it's going to be in the house, we should all know how to be safe around it."

Ronan took his job teaching us about gun safety very seriously, and it wasn't long before I had competition from my entire family over who had the biggest crush on Ronan. Lucas had even started flipping his nonexistent bangs out of his eyes the way Ronan did.

"All right," said Ronan. "Do you guys have any ear protection?"

We had only Dad's old pair of earmuffs for the lawnmower and a slightly scuzzy pair of earplugs Mom brought from her bathroom. It meant that only one person could be out shooting with Ronan at a time. I volunteered to go before Mom could say something embarrassing.

"Let's go out in the pasture," said Ronan. "Sorry, Lucas, but only people with hearing protection should come near, and we need to know you're out of range."

"We'll keep him here," said Mom. "Have fun!" Mom winked at me unbearably, and I knew she was imagining every romantic movie where they have a scene with the guy putting his arms around the lady to show her how to do something.

We walked out to the pasture together, and Ronan set up nine tin cans on the fence. I gave the earmuffs to Ronan and gingerly stuffed the earplugs in my ears.

"Okay," said Ronan. "You want the butt of the rifle right in the meaty part of your shoulder because it's going to kick back." He showed me on himself and then handed me the rifle. It was heavier than I thought it would be, and the wood was warm. I waited until Ronan was standing behind me and then raised the gun and looked down the barrel.

"Good," said Ronan. "Just move that hand. . . ." Ronan tugged awkwardly at my left hand and then moved the butt of the gun, but it wasn't working. "Sorry," he said. And then he put his arms around me, just like they do in the movies. I got so distracted that I let the front of the rifle drop, and when Ronan lunged to catch it, he knocked me forward. It wasn't so much like it is in the movies.

Eventually we got it sorted out and Ronan loaded two cartridges into the rifle.

"All right," he said, grinning. "Blast away."

I raised the rifle and nestled the butt into the inside of my shoulder. I adjusted my hand on the stock and then found the sights and aimed toward the first can. The earplugs blocked out enough noise that it made my other senses sharper. I felt my eyes focus and my breath slow, and it all sort of fell into place with a click. I breathed out and pulled the trigger.

I must have winced when the gun went off, because the can just disappeared. Ronan whooped behind me. I raised the gun, aimed, and shot the second can, this time sending it twirling into the air. Ronan punched me in the shoulder and grinned again. I reloaded the rifle and went down the line nine for nine, hitting every one. I wouldn't have guessed it, but I am a dead shot.

# Chapter Twenty-Three: 807 Miles

### Caleb

The next day Dad and I sail like we've been doing it all our lives. It's almost like it's our duty to be great sailors now that Doc is gone. We get the feel for how to turn the rudder to steer the boat and how to let out the sails so that we don't go too fast and we don't tip over. Then we figure out how to do both at the same time, so that the steering helps the sailing and vice versa. We take turns even, now that it's just Dad and me, so Dad can relax and stretch out his muscles. Dad takes longer turns, but I bring him food and water and sunscreen, and he talks to me about stuff I never knew before. It's like when Dad is sailing, he forgets that he hates to talk, like he's reading words off the water that rushes by.

He tells me about his sister, my aunt Karen, how smart she was and how she wanted to grow up to be really rich and powerful and famous.

"What happened?" I ask. "I mean, how come she ended up just being a mom in Vermont?"

"I don't know, really," says Dad, "but she met your uncle and I think she just fell in love."

"So she gave it all up?"

"I think she thought your uncle was going to become rich and famous for her. Or maybe she didn't expect that she'd have kids so soon, but it seems to me that she never really forgave Uncle Alan for not having bigger plans for himself."

I study my dad to reassure myself that it is really my dad who is, well, *gossiping* with me.

"Mom says that Uncle Alan comes from a rich family, but it's not as rich as Aunt Karen pretends it is."

Dad grunts. "Far as I can tell, money causes more problems than it solves. Makes you think you deserve things you don't need."

"Yeah, but you're sailing a yacht, Dad."

Dad grins and scrubs the top of my head. "Your aunt Karen would probably sell a kidney to be on this boat."

We don't know where we are, but it doesn't matter because we just keep the coast of Michigan to our right. At night Dad sails as long as he can stay awake, then he uncleats the sails and pushes a gear. A motor turns on that sucks the sails up into the boom. Finally, he puts out the anchor, since we're not in such deep water anymore and everything quiets and he sleeps without moving until dawn.

After breakfast Dad pulls up the anchors, I push the gear, and the sails grow magically out of the boom. We tie everything into place and we're off again.

The next day is pretty much the same, except the wind is a little stronger, and I am glad we had a day to practice when it wasn't so windy. Twice the boat tips so much that the motorcycle slides across the floor on its side and leaves huge scratches on the deck.

"Sorry, Doc!" Dad shouts into the wind, and then he tells me to tie down the bike so it won't slide around.

One really great thing about this whole trip is that Dad doesn't treat me like a kid anymore. He *can't* stop sailing to tie up the motorcycle, so I *have* to do it, and I do. It's not fancy knots or anything, but even when we almost tip over again, that motorcycle doesn't move an inch.

That afternoon we pass under a huge, high bridge, which Dad says must be the Mackinac Bridge, so we are at the tip of Michigan. The bridge is just packed with cars. It looks like everybody in Michigan is trying to get north into Canada.

Now we have a different plan for navigating. We have to keep the islands and shore of the Upper Peninsula on our left, but far away, since we don't have charts of the bottom and Dad is worried we're going to hit a shallow spot if we go in too close. I ask him why he wasn't worried yesterday.

"I just didn't think of it yesterday," he says. I frown and then grin.

About an hour before sunset it is still windy, and there are whitecaps racing alongside of us like they're trying to get ahead. I feel deaf after a whole day of standing in the wind, and tired, too, because you have to pay attention every second.

"Caleb!" My dad calls me to the back of the boat. I have my sea legs now and I hop over the motorcycle with no trouble, even though the deck of the boat heaves up and down and is slippery from spray.

"Hey, Dad." I have to almost shout to be heard.

"It's a pretty good wind still, so we've got to decide if we keep going or try to find a place to park. I don't know if we should trust the anchor in this wind."

"You mean keep going all night?"

"Yeah, I don't think we should try to go close to shore without being able to see what the bottom looks like, so we've got to do it now while it's still light out or not at all."

"Aren't you tired?" I ask.

"If you make me some of your famous coffee, I'll be all right." Dad grins at me, but it looks like there are extra lines of tiredness around his eyes.

"I could take a shift if you want." I try to look really competent when I say this, but just then we hit a really big wave and I stumble sideways.

Dad smiles at me. "I think I'll be fine if you just hold our course for three minutes so I can use the head."

"The head" is the toilet in boat language, so I nod and squeeze my way behind Dad so that I can take the tiller. It's the fourth time I've given Dad a break today, but this time the tiller feels like it's alive. It moves like something is under the boat grabbing it, so I pull it tight. We swerve and the sails catch even more wind, so we tilt and shoot forward at the same time. I let it out a little and we slant back, but now my heart is trying to pound its way out of my chest.

"You got it?" Dad asks.

I nod and take a wider stance for balance. I force myself to relax the hand that is holding the tiller, and I look to the left to check our distance from the shore. Even this far away I can tell that we are speeding along, and the trees and rocks and land are just flickering by. It's like when you are running really fast and you don't even feel it, those few seconds when your muscles don't hurt and your lungs don't burn and you're just cruising as fast as you can.

After a few minutes Dad pokes his head out of the hatch and gives me a thumbs-up. I grin at him to let him know I'm fine, so he ducks back into the hold and I stand on the deck, wishing that girl from the boat that got pirated could see me now. I wish Doc could see me too, but maybe he can if he's in heaven or something.

168

After about half an hour my arm feels like it weighs a hundred pounds and the outsides of my legs are hurting from bracing against the swells. I'm still grinning when Dad comes to take the tiller, but just because I'm so proud of myself. Dad tells me to go inside to eat some dinner, since there is so much spray coming up over the edges of the boat that I can't eat on deck like we usually do. I check on Dad one last time, then head downstairs to eat. Dad made pasta and left my bowl in the bottom of the little sink because the boat is moving about so much he didn't want it to slide off the counter. I eat with my left hand, since my right one is still so tired from holding on to the tiller. I think that maybe I will read in bed for a while, but before I even read one page, I am sound asleep.

I am having a really great dream where I'm flying and it's sort of like swimming the breaststroke. I do one stroke forward and soar up in the air, and then sink as the stroke finishes. Up and down I bob through the air over the soccer field at home. I do two, three strokes in a row and get really high, then sink again. I'm six feet over the grass and about to do another stroke to get higher when BAM! I hit the ground.

I wake up and it turns out I've fallen out of bed and hit the floor, except it's not the floor, it's the lower part of the wall because the boat is almost on its side. The boat tips violently and this time I hit the floor, roll like an empty bottle, and crash into the side of the bed. I splay out my arms and legs like a starfish, so that when the boat tips again, I slide back toward the wall but catch myself on my feet.

Now that I am awake, I cannot believe that I was sleeping. The boat heaves and slams and I can hear things crashing out of cupboards and rolling around on the floor.

"Dad!" I yell. Luckily, when I fell asleep reading, I left the light on, so I can see when I jumble to my hands and knees and scramble across the floor. When I get to the doorway, I notice handles at waist height that I never saw before. I grab one and haul myself up, then stagger out into the main cabin. In the kitchen one of the cupboards is slamming open and shut, and all the plates and bowls that were inside are now rolling and sliding across the floor. A wave of water sluices down the steps, splashes across the floor, and makes the carpet swell and gleam. It slows to a trickle, and then a fresh wave splashes down and I get soaked.

"Dad!" I yell again.

I recognize the sound of the engine and I try to think. Dad must be up on deck driving the boat. How can I help? What should I do? Another wave pours down the hatch into the kitchen, and that gives me my first clue. I've got to close the hatch. I grab both handrails and haul myself up the slippery stairs toward the deck. The boat is rocking so viciously that I have to jam my feet inside the steps to keep from falling off sideways. The second my head pokes up above the hatch, the wind snatches my hair like it's trying to scalp me and then I get drenched again by another wave.

It's quiet inside the wave, but the quiet only lasts a second and then there is just a blanket of noise. I blink water out of my eyes and catch a glimpse of Dad. His face is lit in green light from the control panel and he's wearing a life vest. Then another wave comes and knocks me back down into the kitchen.

I lurch up the ladder again, grab the handle and get it about one third closed before another wave. I fight against the water, and when the boat slams to the other side, I yank the hatch shut and fall forward onto the ladder. It's quieter now, and since I'm not getting drenched every five seconds, I can think. I need to help Dad, but what can I do? I can stay down here inside the boat, not knowing whether my dad is washed overboard or still driving the boat, or I can go out there and try not to get swept over the side myself. It doesn't take me long to decide.

I find a life vest and a long piece of rope. The life vest is too big and it keeps knocking me under the chin, but it's better than nothing. I tie a little loop in one end of the rope and then tie the other end around my waist. I don't give myself much time to think about it; I just yank open the hatch, fit my loop of rope around a cleat on the floor, and crawl out into the storm. Staying low to the deck and hanging on to the cleat, I manage to get the hatch closed behind me.

I am on my hands and knees and I look around. I can see that Dad has tied himself to the helm with a big, messy collection of knots. The motorcycle, incredibly, is still where I tied it this morning. Dad shouts something that gets carried off in the teeth of the wind, but if I had to guess, he was telling me to get down below. I slither toward him until I can grab his leg, then tie myself up next to him. Standing up is like trying to climb a greased pole, but I make it. I squint through the spray and see that we are driving south east at full throttle, which puts us almost sideways to the wind. Every two seconds another wave sluices across the deck, but the spray and the wind are constant.

"A little while longer!" shouts my dad. The deck heaves and slaps below us. I can see that the mainsail is down, but the jib, the smaller sail at the front of the boat, is still two-thirds of the way up. I point at it and Dad yells, "Stuck!" Lightning illuminates the thrashing waves for a second. They are as tall as my dad, driving at the side of our boat.

I watch the waves, as if by keeping an eye on them, I can intimidate them enough to keep them from sweeping over us. So I am looking right at it when suddenly the water sucks away from us in a huge, sweeping valley. My eyes travel up the side of the water, which is veined in foam, and there is a wave that is as tall as my dad's house.

"Dad!" I scream, pointing. We tip down into the trough of the water below the monster wave and the wind dies ominously. Dad spins the steering wheel and the boat swerves like a face trying to avoid a slap. The enormous wave tips us forward, and then Dad drops to the deck next to me, throws some loops of rope around the helm, and wraps me and the helm in an iron-hard bear hug.

We are in the wave.

I hear gurgling, deadened and quieter after the howling wind. I am holding my dad's waist and the water lifts my legs up off the deck. I slide down my dad's body and start to sluice out the bottom of the too-big life vest, all the while twisting and bumping like a shirt in the wind. Finally the water drains away and I am dropped to the deck again.

I am so far into the life vest that I can hear my own gasps echoing around in the hollow. I still have the fingers of one hand hanging on to Dad's pant leg, and I use his pants to haul myself into a kneeling position.

Dad is on his front with one arm wrapped in a tangle of ropes and the second hanging on to the top of my life vest.

Our eyes lock briefly and then another wave washes around the deck.

Dad starts to cackle and I think for a minute that he's lost his mind, but the cackle is contagious and I start to laugh, half crying, as I find my feet again.

We scramble weakly to our feet, and my knees are so jittery I can barely stand.

The motorcycle is gone and one of the seats that is screwed to the deck is tipped sideways.

"Hang on!" shouts Dad, so I sit and wrap my arms around a railing. Dad turns the boat so that now the wind is behind us and then cuts the engine. The jib snaps out and we lurch forward, racing the wind. The deck stops heaving side to side and starts lurching up and down like a bronco, but it's better, less chaotic and not as loud.

"Had to steer away from the coast," shouts Dad. "I can't see a thing!"

It's true; we are flying along as fast as we've ever sailed, in total darkness. The light at the bow shows me nothing but twenty feet of black, surging water.

"If we crash, this is going to kill us," I shout, tugging at the ropes that we've used to tie ourselves to the helm. If the helm broke off and sank, we'd be stuck right with it.

"Tie yourself to me," yells Dad.

I work at the knots with fingers that are slippery and stiff with cold. It's hard to keep track of which rope leads where, but eventually I untie Dad and me from the helm. I retie a loop around his waist, then play out thirty feet of rope and tie the other end around me. I give Dad a thumbs-up.

"It's you and me, bub!" Dad shouts. There is a twist of water playing off his chin like a rope of drool. He looks savage and invincible in the green light of the control panel.

"And Doc," I yell, pointing up at the sky.

Dad cackles and lets go of the steering wheel with one hand, sweeping his arm out to the wind. He howls. I howl. We go howling off into the night.

# Chapter Twenty-Four: Miracle #3

## Leah

When Leah woke up, it took her a minute to identify the feeling that fluttered between her shoulder blades like wings. It was excitement. Why was she excited? Because of the wiring. She'd figured out the problem, and today they were going to hike to the next hut and find some wire to replace the chewed part.

Leah opened her eyes and stared at the wooden ceiling, which was only a few feet over her head. She listened.

"Sam?" she whispered.

"Hey."

Leah scooted herself over to the edge of the bed in her sleeping bag and peered over the side. "Hey," she whispered back.

Sam grinned up at her from the bunk below. "How'd you sleep?"

"Great," said Leah. "Really good, actually."

"Me too," said Sam. "I like these guys."

"Yeah. It's like summer camp."

"Better. Amazing food and no jerks."

Leah laughed and swung her legs over the edge. "What do you think Chunk is cooking for breakfast?"

Sam sniffed the air. "Pancakes?"

"No way! I haven't had pancakes since . . ." Leah couldn't remember. Pancakes were something innocent that had been lost to her since Janie died. No, it was before that. Her dad had just stopped making them for some reason.

"Hey, guys," said Chunk, poking his head into the bunk room. "You want chocolate chips in your pancakes?"

Leah smiled. "Just tell it to me straight. Have I died? Is this heaven?"

"Don't let it go to your head, Chunk," shouted Scoggin. His mouth sounded full. "She doesn't know that you snore."

Leah and Sam joined Scoggin and Bear at a table in the dining room. There was a stack of steaming-hot pancakes in the middle of the table, and Scoggin and Bear were eating them three at a time. Chunk sprinkled pinches of mini chocolate chips into a dozen pancakes on the griddle with majestic flair. Soon Screech slouched into the dining room and stared dully at the tabletop. Rainy came in and pushed Screech gently to a bench, then brought her a cup of coffee. Screech sipped it, winced, and then got up and went over to a table that had sugar and creamer on it and poured sugar into her cup. She sipped again, grimaced, and kept on sipping until a little bit of life and intelligence worked their way into her expression.

Rainy looked over at Leah and rolled her eyes. "She's a bit of a slow starter."

Leah watched the whole thing, and everybody else, fascinated. She'd met these people just twenty hours ago, but she wanted to know everything about them.

After everyone had eaten, and Sam and Leah had been walked through the system of dishwashing and the entire kitchen was spotless, Screech came into the kitchen and cleared her throat.

"Alright, so Leah, you and Scoggin are going to Lakes today to scrounge up some more wire." Screech's accent made Leah want to curtsy whenever Screech talked to her. "I thought I'd come along too and see if there is some more food we should bring back. Would you care to join us, Rainy?"

"Sure," said Rainy.

"Okay," said Leah. "far is it to Lakes? Will we be back here tonight?"

Rainy laughed. "It's the next hut over and about seven miles. Nobody is staying there, so we've been using it as our personal supply depot."

"I'll come too," said Bear. "I can do another gas tank."

The four crew members nodded respectfully in a way that made Leah wonder what "do another gas tank" meant. She raised her eyebrows at Rainy.

"Bear can carry a gas tank. By himself. It weighs more than a hundred pounds. No one else can do it."

Bear shrugged, folded up another pancake from a pile of leftovers, and stuffed it into his mouth. "Gotta earn my keep."

The trail to Lake of the Clouds Hut tripped and tumbled its way over rocks that ranged in size from Volkswagens to bread boxes. It was not steep or long, but it was still challenging because your feet were rarely on flat ground. When they got there, Leah saw why the hut crew had chosen to live at Madison instead. Lake of the Clouds Hut was much bigger and could fit twice as many guests. The road that went up to the top of Mount Washington was only a mile away, and Rainy told Leah that the hut was haunted.

Leah and Scoggin stripped several yards of wire out of the wall in the crew room of the hut, and before Leah could even congratulate herself about the achievement, she was headed back

176

to Madison, feeling slightly ridiculous to be carrying two pounds of wire while Bear huffed along under an enormous gas canister that looked like a torpedo the size of Lucas.

It took Leah only another hour to fix the water pump, which earned her the same sort of respect that Bear got for carrying the gas canister and that Chunk got for his flawless brioche. The hut crew were proud of one another's talents but not intimidated. It was really pleasant, actually. At school Leah's brains seemed to alienate her from people. Here it was almost expected.

That evening everybody took showers, hot showers, something Leah would never take for granted again. The scent of shampoo was overwhelming and astringent after only natural smells. The soap made Leah's skin feel so smooth that she was slippery. Her whole body had changed, muscle and bone jutting out in spots she'd never noticed before, the hair on her legs wiry and pointing in every direction. Leah had never hated her body, not like Regan had, but she'd never appreciated it either. Now she was proud of it, proud of what she could do, not what she looked like.

After dinner the crew took Leah and Sam out on a spit of rocks that jutted into the emptiness over a deep valley. It felt like standing on a diving board in the middle of the sky. Everyone found a spot to sit and squinted into the sun until it set. Leah heard quiet, appreciative murmuring as the stippled clouds became splashed with fuchsia and gold. She let the sounds and the feeling wash over her like warm water.

"Only in nature would those two colors look good together," said Rainy. She was kneading Bear's shoulder with her fists.

"Thanks, Rainy," Bear rumbled. "Can you do my back?"

"Sure. Let's go inside, though."

Rainy and Bear got up to leave, and Screech, Scoggin, and Chunk stood up too.

"You two coming in?" asked Chunk.

"In a bit," said Leah.

"Soon," said Sam.

The sounds of the crew going back to the hut faded behind them, and Leah shifted around to find a more comfortable spot on the broad, sloped rock she shared with Sam.

"You have a good day?" Leah asked Sam.

"Yeah. It was great, actually. Chunk taught me how to make bread."

"That's awesome. Your bread was really good, you know."

"Thanks. Nice job on the water pump. Genius."

Leah grinned and nudged Sam's shoe with her foot.

Sam hugged himself and shifted on the rocks. "This was probably the best day of my life."

Leah nodded. "It was pretty good." She frowned. "But really, the best day of your life? We're in the middle of some kind of apocalypse, you know."

"Definitely the best day of my life." Sam swallowed and stared determinedly into the fading sunset.

"Well, I guess that this is the best day since . . . since I killed my best friend."

"You really think you killed your friend? Even with the burn?"

"What?" Leah peered at Sam through the growing darkness. "What burn?"

"On your collarbone." Sam touched Leah's right collarbone gently with his finger. "It's a burn, right? Like some kind of rope burn."

Leah stared at Sam, feeling like something, some energy, was prickling around the base of her spine. It was the same feeling she got when she was about to figure something out with the machines she invented in her head, as if the answer were coalescing out of the air behind her.

"What?" she said again.

"It's a burn from your seat belt. It's on the right side. Where the passenger-side seat belt would be."

Leah felt like she'd been falling through space for the past year and had just landed with a huge crash. She shook her head, as if she could rattle the ringing sound out of it.

"You didn't figure that out?" asked Sam. "I'm right, aren't I? I should have told you right away, but I thought you knew. I thought you were being tough or something. You weren't driving that car."

"I . . ." Leah lay back suddenly on the rock and looked up at the first few stars. She searched for Sam's hand next to her, and he squeezed hers. Tears leaked down the sides of Leah's face into her ears.

"I can't remember anything." Leah's voice was a hoarse whisper. "Just her profile, laughing, but . . . they kept asking me who was driving, and I couldn't remember, so I said I was—I said it was my fault." Leah closed her eyes, holding back a sob. "But it's real, then. I remember the right side of her face all lit up green by the dash lights. I didn't do it."

Sam studied the side of Leah's face, a little nervous.

"For a genius, you're pretty dumb," he said. He touched her scar again.

"Sam," she whispered, "I think you just saved my life. Again."

Sam patted her awkwardly on the shoulder in the darkness.

"Hey," said Leah.

179

"What?" said Sam.

"Let's go home."

# Chapter Twenty-Five: Sugar

### Margot

Lucas and Ronan and I were out by the side of the house scrubbing a *huge* pile of laundry in the washtub.

"I can't believe this was considered 'women's work,'" I said, a little out of breath. "This is a serious workout."

"I wish it still was considered women's work," grumbled Ronan.

I flicked some water at him and he grinned.

"Aren't you, like, my mom's slave? I should make you do this by yourself."

Ronan shrugged. "Fine. I'll be the one with the amazing biceps."

"You are the one with the amazing biceps," I muttered under my breath. I think that from the way Ronan grinned at me again, he heard or guessed what I'd said.

I had turned away with a basket full of wet laundry to hang on the line when I heard the barking. Five dogs trotted in a pack down the driveway at the front of the house and headed for the garden in the front lawn.

"Git outta here!" I shouted. The beans we'd planted had already sent up little bright-green elbows, which Grandma expected to open up into leaves soon. I put the basket down and stomped toward the dogs. Two of them—rangy, thin dogs with pointed ears—barked at me and capered sideways into the garden, trampling the little beans.

I didn't even stop to think. I ran in the back door and yanked the gun off the top of the refrigerator. I stepped out the front door and confronted the dogs.

"Get!" I shouted. The two barked at me again, scornfully. Two others circled distrustfully, and the last was a chubby-looking black Lab that sat down and panted with his eyes rolling. The two barkers started to run in a playful circle through the center of the garden, sending up sprays of our precious dirt. "Stop it!" I shouted. I loaded the gun, took aim, and shot into the air over their heads.

It was too much for the Lab. He yelped and waddled back down the driveway, but the other four dogs were intimidated only for a second. They trotted in a loose formation out of the garden and around the side of the house. Ronan was halfway between me and where we had been scrubbing the laundry. Behind him was Lucas, sitting by a pile of dirty laundry looking very small and vulnerable. And there were the chickens frozen in postures of curiosity.

The lead dog dropped its ears back over its skull and hunched into a low, crouching trot, eyes locked on the closest chicken. The other dogs did the same, spreading out to either side.

I had seen animals do this in National Geographic shows about predators and prey, so I didn't even pause. I lowered the muzzle of the rifle, aimed a few inches in front of the lead dog, let out my breath, and pulled the trigger. The dog spun away from me like it had been yanked by a leash, and dropped to the ground, its back legs sliding sideways. The other dogs yipped and scrambled away down the hill.

I put the rifle on the ground and ran toward Lucas. He was as white as the T-shirt he was holding, and his breath came in loud pants. I scooped him up and ran with him back into the house.

Mom came running into the kitchen, saw me holding Lucas, and grabbed him out of my arms.

"What happened? What happened to my baby?"

"I'm fine, Mom. It was dogs. Margot shot them." Lucas looked at me and tears sprouted in his eyes. "You shot it, Margot. A dog."

I gaped at Lucas and then at Mom, who narrowed her eyes at me.

"They were after the chickens," I said, looking at Lucas, absorbing the frightened glare he was giving me from the safety of Mom's arms.

Then it hit me like a smack across the face. I had just shot a dog.

I turned and whirled out the back door, tripping and stumbling down the hill to the smoker. I collapsed onto a fallen log and stared into the burned-out trunk of the tree. It was just as hollow and cold as I felt.

"Hey." Ronan's voice was a soft breath.

I turned and looked up at him, tears streaming down my cheeks.

"You all right?" he asked, moving cautiously to stand in front of me.

I shook my head miserably and Ronan sat down next to me.

His arm was just a millimeter from mine. It felt like every little hair on my arm was reaching out to him.

"Hey," he said again. He touched a tear on my cheek. "Don't cry, Margot." He sounded so forlorn that I laughed, which only made more tears squirt out. Ronan gently turned my face toward him and wiped the new tears away with his thumbs.

"I just shot a dog, Ronan. A pet."

"You only did what their owners should have done. I heard about a family who used up their last gallon of gas to drive their dog off and abandon it. It's not like there is any hope of those dogs surviving."

"But," I sobbed, "I love dogs."

"Well, you did it a kindness. The rest are all probably going to starve to death slowly in the next weeks. You did the right thing."

"My chickens . . ." I couldn't figure out what I wanted to say.

"They're back to eating bugs."

"I'm sorry." I sniffed again, feeling very tired and sad.

Ronan was quiet while I wiped my nose on the bottom of my shirt.

"That was amazing, you know." He smiled hesitantly. "You're, like, some kind of sharpshooter."

Another sob sent a fresh gush of tears down my cheeks.

"Honest. I never saw anyone shoot like that." Ronan wiped my face again, and this time I looked up at him.

His eyes wrinkled into another smile and he licked his bottom lip.

It was the lip that did it.

I leaned in and he leaned in and we were sharing the air between us. His fingers worked into the hair at the back of my head, and I grabbed his arms and felt the muscles there, moving under his skin, and then my lips met his lips, scalding and smooth and every bit as delicious as I had ever imagined.

# Chapter Twenty-Six: 524 Miles

### Caleb

At some point the sky goes from thick, deep black to icy steel gray to soft, misty gray the exact color of my exhaustion. My clothes are damp and I appear to be sitting in a puddle on the deck. I look down at my hands and see white puckered skin, pink watery blood, and oozing blisters. I have to concentrate to open my fingers one by one from around the rope I've been holding all night.

"We need coffee, bub," says Dad. The sound of his voice makes me jerk. "Make yourself something hot to drink and get into some dry clothes."

I stand up and all my joints feel like they're put together with rusty bolts. I creep across the deck like an old man and fumble with the hatch for a good minute before I can get my hands to work well enough to force it open.

My hands are too sore to hang on to the ladder, so I half jump, half fall into the kitchen and land in about half an inch of water. The plates and bowls lie scattered about the floor, looking like polka dots to my tired eyes. I step around it all and go to Doc's room, manage to open the closet, and find some clothes. It takes some doing, but eventually I am dressed in dry clothes and have gauze wrapped around both hands from the first-aid kit. It takes me another half hour to make coffee and hot cocoa, and then I have to figure out how to carry Dad's mug up the ladder without using my hands too much.

I pull a pair of Doc's socks over my hands for extra protection and then grab some clothes for Dad and a towel and bring it all up on deck.

Dad moves like he's made of rusty parts too. His hands are worse than mine, way worse. When he unpeels them from the steering wheel, two huge flaps of skin on his palms rip open and start bleeding. Without saying anything, I go back down and get the first-aid kit and some more socks, and then I do up Dad's hands as best I can.

Dad takes off his wet shirt. I notice that you can see all the outlines of his muscles and ribs. The rubbery pouch that used to bulge over the top of his pants is gone. He looks like he should be in an advertisement for men's deodorant or something, except that he has huge sock paws on each hand. Mom always says I'm going to be just as handsome as my dad, but she always makes it sound like that's a bad thing.

I bring Dad his coffee, and after he takes a sip, he points his paw over my shoulder. I look and see a little wrinkle on the horizon. Land.

"That's east," says Dad. "It's Canada, but I don't know what part. I say we head that way and find out where we are."

Dad and I drink about five cups of hot drink and eat our way through two cans of nuts, a box of granola bars, and three jars of martini olives. When neither one of us can eat or drink another thing, Dad sends me below decks and tells me that he'll wake me up when we get closer to land.

It seems like I just closed my eyes when I feel Dad climb into the bed next to me.

186

"I dropped the anchor," he says by way of explanation, then he pulls up the covers, rolls over, and goes right to sleep.

When I wake up, yellow light is slanting in through the tiny window at the top of our room. I look over at Dad, but he is limp and boneless, as if he were dropped into the bed from a great height. I roll carefully out of the side of the bed so that I don't wake him up, and tiptoe out of the room.

Up on the deck I touch a deep gouge that marks the last trace of our motorcycle. I wobble the deck chair and see where four of the bolts holding it into place have bent backward and the other four have disappeared. The bolts are each as thick as my thumb.

I look back to the west and squint across the lake. The water looks like a piece of steel that has dimples pounded into it, and there are fluffy white clouds scuttling across the sky. The world looks so safe and inviting that last night seems like a half-remembered nightmare.

To the east I can see a long wooded shore and gentle hills. We are close enough for me to make out a few small houses and docks, but not so close that we are parked in anyone's way. After being on the boat for so long it feels like home. I'm not really sure I want to leave it behind and go to Vermont.

Dad comes up on deck behind me and stretches so long that I hear a number of things pop in his back. He has brought up a jar of tiny pickles and another jar of olives. I open them for him without having to be asked. He puts a plate on the deck and then dumps both jars out onto the plate, so that the juice runs off the sides. We eat again, looking at the shore.

"I say let's head to that dock with the little blue rowboat," says Dad. He lifts a paw toward the shore.

187

There is a small brown house with a lawn that slopes steeply down to the water. I can just make out a person—a man, I think—who is out on the lawn. He moves a few feet and stoops over then walks again and bends. He looks like he's picking up something off his lawn, but it's too far away to tell.

"Looks good to me," I say.

We anchor our boat as near to the dock as we can get and then call to the man, who has an armload of branches. I guess the storm was bad here too. The next thing I know he has rowed us to his dock in the little blue rowboat and his wife is making us hot tea in huge brown mugs and they are asking if we really survived the storm out in the middle of the lake. Dad has remembered that he doesn't talk much, so it's up to me to tell them about the pirates and Doc and the wave as big as Dad's house and how we're trying to get to Vermont. Without even realizing it, I eat through three bowls of lentil soup, which normally I hate.

We learn that we are in Skookumchuck, a tiny town in Canada that is about a one-day drive from Vermont. Maggie is the woman; she has a long gray braid and boobs that hang all the way to the waistband of her shorts. You can tell from her face she smiles a lot, so I like her even though she wears socks with her sandals. Scott is the man. He is stooped and thin, but not as old as Grandma. He tells Dad he's from Maryland, but he came up to Canada in 1967. I can tell that is code for something because Dad nods respectfully, but I don't know what.

"We didn't get the blackouts up here, but we got hit by the virus, all right," says Scott.

"What virus is that?" Dad asks. He pulls back from the table and wipes his mouth carefully.

Maggie laughs. "You two really have been out in the middle of a lake."

"Computer virus," says Scott. "Any gadget that was connected to the Internet got it. Phones, GPS, anything. The virus literally melted the guts of everything it touched."

"Melted how?" asked Dad.

"Heat. As far as anyone knows, most of the gadgets in the world are completely useless and unrepairable. The most sophisticated technology we have is a calculator!"

I can tell by the way he's talking that Scott is secretly delighted that computers have all been melted. I can also tell that he doesn't know that much about technology because of how he explained the virus.

"So the virus destroyed every computer's cooling system or it did something else?" I ask.

Everyone looks at me blankly.

"Don't know, don't care," says Scott. "Maggie misses her shows, but we do just fine without all that stuff."

Maggie looks like she disagrees, but she just offers me another slice of bread.

"Half of the United States is trying to get into Canada or Mexico," says Maggie. "They certainly have a different view of immigrants and refugees now." Maggie sniffs to show she doesn't think much of Americans.

"They know who did it yet?" asks Dad.

"Only rumors," says Scott, "but the most consistent rumor is that it's the army or part of the army with the help of some left-wing folks." Again Scott cannot quite conceal his glee. I start to get a little nervous because I know that Dad thinks that liberals should mind their own business.

"Can't say I'll miss that president of yours," cackles Scott.

"Lying, racist misogynist . . . ," Maggie mutters.

"What happened to him?" asks Dad.

"He quit!" crows Scott. "He hopped on a jet and flew off with a hold full of beauty pageant contestants!"

The president has always reminded me of the bullies from the 1980s high school movies I watched with Mom. He seems like the kind of guy who people like only because he's rich. I hope nobody likes him now that he isn't president anymore.

The grown-ups start talking about politics stuff, and suddenly I can barely hold up my head. The next thing I know, Dad is pulling a blanket up under my chin with his big sock paws and I go to sleep without dreaming.

# Chapter Twenty-Seven: Mistake?

### Leah

The crew from Madison Hut radioed ahead to the crew at Mizpah to warn them that Sam and Leah were on their way through. When they got to Mizpah, Leah understood Screech's vague warning that "they're taking this whole thing pretty seriously."

Josh, a tall blond with a buzz cut that looked self-inflicted, met them at the spur trail to the hut wearing full forest camo and holding a crossbow. He asked them security questions, some of which they knew how to answer (where Screech was from) and some they didn't (Rainy's real name). In the end, it might have been pity that moved him to let them come into the hut, because it had been raining for the past half hour and Leah started to shiver as they stood there on the trail.

The Mizpah crew had certainly taken a different approach to the blackouts than the Madison crew had. There was a chart on the refrigerator that described everybody's rations for the week, and they had begun to fill the dining room with wood for the stove. Leah was both horrified and impressed when she learned that they had bucked all the wood with a bow saw.

Three of the four hut crew members were boys from Colby College who had rowed crew together. They'd all gotten jobs in the huts for the summer, and when they heard about the blackouts, they joined up at Mizpah.

"I was on my days off when it happened," said Tavia, the only girl. "I was with my folks in Ipswich, Mass., and it got bad really fast. Whoever did this fried everything that was connected to the Internet."

"Fried how?" asked Leah. She hadn't heard that part of it before.

Tavia shrugged. "My dad has this really old laptop, and after it got the virus, it just heated up until it actually singed the kitchen table at home!"

"So you mean it was literally fried? With heat?"

"Yeah," said Tavia. "My iPhone, too. I tried to open it up and check the battery, but something inside had melted."

"Whoa," said Leah. "I guess that means things are going to take longer to fix than I thought."

Tavia nodded. "My folks think that the government is going to save them, but I didn't want to wait around for that. We are way better off up here than everybody I saw down there." "Down there" seemed to be her term for everywhere that wasn't the mountains.

"We've got it figured out," said Tom, an Asian American from New York. "We're taking apart the woodstove from Zealand and moving it here piece by piece."

"You have enough food to last all winter?" asked Leah.

Tom looked at the other three crewmates. Josh nodded solemnly.

"If we're careful," said Tavia.

"Can't you find a real saw somewhere?" asked Sam, holding up the flimsy bow saw with one hand. "I can't believe you cut all this wood with this little saw."

192

"Nah," said Josh. "We're not going down there unless we have to."

Part of their survival plan depended on hunting and trapping, a skill they were attempting to learn from a tattered old book. That night they ate a squirrel stew that could have used a little of Chunk's flair. Tavia was very proud, since it was the first thing she'd caught in one of her traps.

"They make it sound so easy in books!" she laughed ruefully.

"It's great," said Sam. "Better than Mr. Tanden's protein powder, anyway." Sam and Leah shared a smile.

The next morning Leah and Sam ate some oatmeal that Tavia had measured to the last flake, and then hiked out into a slow drizzle that lasted all day. They passed by Zealand Falls Hut, which was locked, and then up a very steep climb to a ridgeline that might have been beautiful if they'd been able to see through the fog and rain.

They reached Galehead Hut at midafternoon and found that that was locked too.

"Do you want to break in a window or something?" asked Sam. He stood under the porch roof, trying to peer inside.

"Let's keep going," said Leah, looking out at the rain. "I am so wet it just doesn't matter anymore, but if I stop, I'll never get going again."

Sam nodded, flipped up the hood on the rain jacket he'd gotten from the abandoned packs, and stepped off the porch back into the rain.

Leah pulled up her own hood and followed Sam. She thought again about how these blackouts had happened. She knew that the nation's power grid was actually a collection of large grids, each separate from the others. Each grid was somewhat vulnerable because it had to be balanced so that the amount of power being used matched the amount of power being created. If you suddenly stopped drawing power or if you suddenly made too much power, the grid would be overwhelmed and go down. Leah wondered if the computers that monitored the power grids were connected to the Internet. If so, and they had all melted, it would take a very long time indeed before the power came back on. It certainly answered one question she'd had about why phones had stopped working too. The attackers hadn't needed to target each service provider or go after cell towers or satellites. By spreading a virus over the Internet, they'd probably melted enough of the crucial hardware to make everything fail. Her own phone hadn't melted because it had been offline when the virus was launched. By the time she'd tried to connect to the Internet, any network that could have given her the virus had already shut down.

What about landlines? The landlines should still work, unless the computers that ran the switchboards had been compromised. Or, thought Leah, they just couldn't work without power.

Leah turned these thoughts over in her head, concentrating so deeply that she was surprised to discover that the seven miles to Greenleaf Hut had passed beneath her feet with no more thought than if she were on a treadmill.

The door of the hut had a hole in it where somebody had forced the lock. If Leah had to guess, some folks had hiked up from the interstate highway and raided the hut, not caring what sort of shape they left it in. It was spooky and unsettling to see a hut ransacked when every other one they'd seen had been scrupulously cared for.

"Do you have the feeling that 'civilization' is bad?" asked Sam. "Like, everything's gone totally crazy while we were up here in the mountains?"

Leah kicked a pillow out of the kitchen, revealing a nest of ants underneath. "I know what you mean. I wish we could just hike through the woods right up to my house." She stopped and studied a map that was pinned to the wall of the hut.

"Actually, I'm kind of excited. Look." Leah pointed with her pinkie to where they were on the map. "It's just a short hike tomorrow morning, then we're out on the interstate. That's about a forty-five-minute drive to my house."

Sam grunted and started pulling off his wet things.

"If we can get a ride to Saint Johnsbury, we can definitely walk the rest of the way in less than a day. Who knows? We could be home for dinner."

Sam looked at her. "Hmm. All this time on the trail and suddenly you're an optimist."

"It's your fault, you know," said Leah, only partially joking. She turned away from the map and shrugged out of her pack. "Seriously, a couple weeks on the trail with you have done more than seven months of a Wiltmore shrink. You're better than my meds."

"It's not me. It's nature and hiking and just being out here." Sam flapped a pair of wet socks to indicate the natural world outside. He paused and looked at the floor. "I think I might keep hiking."

"What?" Leah let her rain pants land on the floor with a wet smack. "You're not going home?"

"No," said Sam. The skittish look that used to haunt Sam's face flickered over his features. "Never."

Sam looked like he was about to say more, but instead he went to work hanging up his socks.

"But you'll come home with me for a little while. Right?" asked Leah.

"Maybe. For a bit."

"Sam." Leah walked over to face him. "How come you were at Wiltmore?"

Sam shook out his raincoat and then hung it between himself and Leah. She couldn't see his face when he said, "It's one of very few year-round boarding schools."

Leah tugged the raincoat aside and smiled at him. "That's not really a recommendation, in my book."

Sam turned away from her, hanging up a pair of rain pants.

"Is if you hate being at home."

"So home is pretty bad, then," said Leah. She noticed the way Sam's shoulders and back had suddenly curved in. "Is it your mom or dad or something?"

Sam wrung out a T-shirt, still not looking at her.

"They're not my real parents. I'm adopted."

Leah waited, listening to the drips of drying clothing.

Sam said nothing more.

# Chapter Twenty-Eight: String's Gone

## Margot

Yesterday my aunt walked down the driveway in the middle of the afternoon. My ex-aunt, I mean, my cousin Caleb's mom. She was really thin and was wearing sneakers that she could not have picked out herself. She didn't say hello or anything, she just asked if Caleb was here or Jerry, and when we said that they weren't, she sort of deflated into a puddle of clothes right there in the driveway. After a few minutes she stood up and said, "Well, put me to work."

I looked at Mom. I thought we should feed her first, but Mom shook her head at me. She took Aunt Alice's hand, walked her out to the woodpile, and put her on the other end of the big crosscut saw.

I followed them and stood watching for a minute. Mom hitched up her pants and I realized that she had lost her pregnant bump. For a second I was surprised she hadn't said anything about it, but only for a second. Each trip down to the post office to check for news of Leah had worn a little more of the veneer away. Sparkle Mom was gone.

Mom and Alice bucked up an entire ash tree. Dad and I split it and Lucas stacked it mostly without talking. It was dark before we stopped for dinner, but our woodpile grew by about eight feet. Mom had to practically carry Aunt Alice inside. She ate without speaking and fell asleep on the couch in the living room.

Aunt Alice was sitting up, holding her forehead in both hands, when I came down the next morning. I brought her a big bowl of oatmeal with nuts and some raisins, and after looking at me like she didn't know who I was, she took the bowl and wolfed it down.

"I walked up from Boston," she said.

Mom and Grandma came and sat on either side of her.

"I called Jerry, and he said he and Caleb were coming here, but I couldn't remember what the name of this town was."

"Canton Hollow," said Lucas.

Aunt Alice smiled at him tiredly.

"I was at the airport, ready to fly to Denver, when things got bad. I couldn't get a rental car because I didn't have cash and the desk was mobbed. I almost got crushed, actually, but Gordan grabbed me."

"Who is Gordan?" asked Mom.

"I didn't know him, but he was black and very tall. He said we needed each other. He was right. We hitched a ride north of Boston thanks to me, and nobody messed with us thanks to him."

"You walked all the way here?" asked Lucas.

"Not all the way. We got a ride through Massachusetts the second day. We had food and water and Gordan's cash still, and there weren't as many people out on the roads looking for help."

Aunt Alice looked up at the ceiling, then closed her eyes.

"Some people tried to help. They gave us water. Somebody gave me a map of Vermont. But some people treated us like we were criminals." Alice stared bitterly into her palms.

"Gordan and I separated in Montpelier. He had an old boyfriend there he was going to stay with. I just thought if I could get here, everything would be okay. I went to Calais first and looked for you, then Cabot. I knew that the town began with *C* and that it was up here somewhere. It was slow going. Roads got worse. People were more desperate. The families . . ." Aunt Alice's eyes filled. "People trying to get food for their children. Women praying for their milk to come back when their babies ran out of formula. I was lucky, really, to have nothing and nobody. But Caleb . . ."

I thought for a minute that Aunt Alice was going to start sobbing and never stop, but she swallowed hard several times and scrubbed her eyes.

"You can stay here," said Grandma.

"But I have nothing!" wailed Aunt Alice. "Literally nothing. I—I stole these shoes out of some abandoned stuff on the side of the road."

Grandma patted Alice's hand and shushed her like a baby. "I know Jeremiah and Caleb are on their way, and I'll bet they'll be here any day. Jeremiah will get them here in one piece."

I had completely forgotten about my uncle and cousin. I rolled the thought of them over in my head, but it couldn't find any purchase. I was too worried about Leah to take on any more.

I left them in the living room and went to check on the beans. The last of our string sagged in sloppy rows. It was stupid to have used it up making markers for the garden. Rain had made it soggy and dirty. I squatted down and picked it out of the dirt, being careful not to disturb the tiny bean plants with their two little leaves reaching to the sky.

My sneakers got soaked in the dew. It occurred to me that I'd better not grow out of them. Like the string, they wouldn't be easy to replace. I had a dozen shoes in my closet that all seemed pretty useless now: plastic flats I'd gotten for a formal, high heels that Judy had pretty much dared me to buy, cheap rain boots with daisies on them. If I ever got to go to a store again, I vowed to buy only things that would last.

I stood up, a little ashamed of my thoughts. Here I was thinking about *things*. I squeezed my fist around the soggy string. I would trade every last piece of clothing in my closet if it meant I could get my sister back.

# Chapter Twenty-Nine: 522 Miles

## Caleb

Three summers ago Dad tried to teach me how to fix a car. I think he thought it would be like when I was a really little kid and I loved to play in the garage with him. Instead I was so miserable that everything he tried to teach me just sort of drizzled out my ear.

So today when Dad and me and Scott go out to the side of Scott's garage and take the tarp off a very old Volkswagen Bug, Dad asks me, sort of shy, if I wouldn't mind helping him out, since his hands are still pretty mangled.

We put in a new battery and a new spark plug, which Scott says about a hundred times is so lucky that he just ordered it last month. We take apart and grease the cylinders and oil everything we can get to. Dad says the timing belt is hanging on by a thread, but that it should get us to Vermont.

We traded Maggie and Scott the boat for the VW, and we all know that Maggie and Scott are getting the better deal, so Maggie is determined to spoil us with food. I can't tell you how good it is to eat real food that somebody cooked in an oven instead of the packaged stuff we've been eating. She makes bread right in her kitchen and she's got chickens, so we eat a bunch of eggs for breakfast and they are the best things I ever ate.

All morning and into the afternoon, Dad points to what bolt needs to be unscrewed and I get the socket wrench and do it, or he explains how to reach into a crevice and use a flathead screwdriver to pop something out and I do. We're a really good team, and a little after lunch Dad lets me climb into the driver's seat, step on the clutch and the gas, and start up the engine.

Scott cheers and says "Groovy, man, groovy" about a hundred times. Dad smiles at me really quiet and proud.

It takes two loads in the rowboat to collect the rest of the food and some other stuff out of Doc's boat. I wrap up Doc's watch and some other valuable-looking stuff and photos to bring to his kid someday. Dad finds some papers that have Doc's address in Chicago, and Nantucket, too. Dad brings Doc's fishing hat. I bring the knife he used to gut the fish. The fastest scalpel in the West. I'm going to keep it if his kid lets me.

Maggie packs up enough food to feed us for three days and squashes me into her bosom so long I start to worry about breathing. Scott tells us for the hundredth time that "the Feds are looking for the license plate on that Bug, man," and then they wave us off, up a steep hill to the road, and once again Dad and I are on our way to Vermont.

Dad drives east for about four hours and I work the gearshift for him. We eat some of what Maggie packed up when we get hungry, and I tell Dad a little bit about school and a little bit about snowboarding, which he's never done, and a little bit about me and Mom in Park City. Dad explains what Scott and Maggie think, which is that the president, who got to be president even though more people voted for the lady, was such a jerk that somebody did all the blackouts and the computer virus to get rid of him. Dad thinks the trouble started before the jerky guy became president, but he says the president probably didn't help. It gets dark slowly, so it takes us a while to realize that the headlights don't work, and we have to make an emergency camp out on the side of the road in flat, open Canada.

In the morning Dad's hands are healed up enough for him to do the shifter, but I don't mind doing it for him. We drive all morning and before lunch we come to the border crossing between Quebec and Vermont.

Our line is only four cars long and the lady working there looks so tired that I think we could be driving a tank, and she'd just wave us through. The line to get into Canada is so long that I can't see the end of it. Every driver has turned off their engine and I see at least a dozen cars being pushed forward. I don't know if they're trying to save gas or they ran out.

We drive into Vermont and I feel a little shiver. We're almost there now.

Dad gives a long whistle as we crest a hill and see the line of cars headed north stretching like a caterpillar out of sight. We drive for twenty minutes before we pass the end of it and you wouldn't believe the amount of stuff there is everywhere. I think of the trailer we left behind and realize that almost everybody had to do the same thing. At some point we all just gave up on stuff and worried about food and family.

Suddenly Dad starts to downshift, and then we're steering down an exit ramp and I notice for the first time how Vermonty everything is, all the green hills and trees and stuff.

I look out the window and I realize that I am expecting to see Mom. I imagine coming up behind her, seeing her red skort that she likes, and pulling over. We'll honk and wave, and when she hugs me, everything will magically go back to normal.

I peer out the window, feeling like my eyes are hungry and that if Mom isn't at Aunt Karen's, I might actually die. I tell myself not to get hopeful, but it's like trying to pop a balloon just by squeezing it. Every time I get one part squished down, hope bursts out the other side.

"Dad, I think I'm having a heart attack. Are we close?"

"Pretty close, buddy."

"What do we do if nobody's there?"

Dad starts to say that our family *will* be there, but I interrupt.

"What if Mom's not there?"

Dad swallows what he was going to say and stares straight ahead. I figure out just then that Dad wants to see Mom almost as much as I do. We took this whole trip just because Dad told her we might come, not because Grandma said to. I narrow my eyes at him. He's changed, a lot really. I look out the window again. If he's excited to see Mom, that's okay with me, I guess.

## Chapter Thirty: Mistakes and Miracles

### Leah

Leah woke in the pale-yellow light of early morning and wondered if today would be the day she made it home. For once she was up and ready before Sam, so she surprised him with breakfast in bed.

"Hey, wake up," she said. She'd found a tray and put an evergreen twig in a vase. A pillowcase stood in for a tablecloth.

"Wow," said Sam, blinking. He sat up in his sleeping bag and scooted back so he could lean against the wall. "What's this for?"

Leah sat on the bunk opposite Sam's and gripped her mug of tea.

"I want you to come home with me."

Sam lifted one corner of his lip—half smile, half question.

"I mean, I'm not going to bring you breakfast in bed every day or anything, but—just . . . come. It's not bad."

Sam blew on a spoonful of oatmeal and studied Leah. "Okay." He shrugged.

"Okay? Really?" Leah stood up. She meant to hug Sam, but the breakfast tray was in the way, so she gave him a funny little pat on his leg instead. "Great. Okay."

Sam seemed immune to Leah's little hints that she was anxious to get going. He carefully stuffed his sleeping bag and tugged on each of the compression straps, some more than once, which was maddening. Leah had never noticed how fussy he was about tying his hiking boots, folding down his socks, pulling each lace straight. When they finally got out on the trail Leah stepped on the back of Sam's boot three times in the first mile.

"Do you want to go ahead?" Sam asked his eyebrow cocked in annoyance.

"No, no, sorry."

The trail was beautiful, following a thin ridge that had long, open views to the north and south. White banners of fog lifted out of the valleys on either side, and each dewy twig and needle glinted in the morning light. Sam paused for a long time at each of the lookouts and then sighed before hiking on. Leah didn't know if he was anxious about leaving the woods or going to her house or what, but she was too wound up to ask.

It was still early when they got down to the road. It was an interstate highway, but the space between the two mountains was too narrow for two lanes in each direction, so the interstate was one lane and had a 45 m.p.h. speed limit. This made it much better for hitchhiking, or would have had there been more traffic.

Leah waited with her thumb out even though there wasn't a car in sight. Sam took off his pack and stretched. After two minutes Leah dropped her thumb and then finally her pack. She did a quad stretch but stopped when she heard a car. It was a Prius that had at least seven people in it. The teenage boy squashed up against the window gave Leah a shrug as they zoomed by.

In the next fifteen minutes two more cars went by. Leah was kicking out her legs and flapping her arms with impatience.

"You look like you're trying to fly home," Sam observed. He imitated Leah's jerky movements.

"I just want to get there, you know?"

Sam nodded. He unpacked a dry T-shirt and was putting it on when a pickup truck came by.

"Sam! It's stopping! Come on!"

Leah lifted her pack and ran up the road to the truck, with her backpack smacking against her leg every other step. The pickup pulled over to the shoulder and the engine cut off. A tall, wiry-looking man dressed all in dirty denim got out and arched his back slightly.

"Hey!" Leah panted. "Thanks for stopping. We're going to Lyndonville or as far as you can take us."

"Lyndonville, huh?" The man stuck his hand down the front of his jeans and scratched. Leah looked away politely.

"We've been walking—"

"We can arrange something." Now the man walked toward Leah. He ran his tongue around in his mouth, upper teeth then lower teeth.

Leah's smile faltered a bit.

"That yer boyfriend?" The man twitched his head toward Sam, who was repacking his pack.

"No, he's—"

"Why don't you and me go for a little walk then."

Leah jerked her head to refuse. Her smile got stuck on her face, more of a grimace now. "No thanks." Some part of her wouldn't believe that this man actually meant what she thought he meant. He kept walking toward her, but Leah stood there waiting for good manners to save her.

He grabbed her bicep in a rough grip and started to propel her toward the trees.

"Hey," said Leah. "Let go. I don't really need a ride, okay?"

Now the man snorted like she'd made a not-very-funny joke, but he didn't let go of her arm. "No such thing as a free lunch, right?"

"What?" Leah dug in her heels and tugged at her arm. "Let go!"

Leah had always thought that she'd have good instincts in a situation like this, but panic and flight seemed slow in coming. It was as if admitting what was happening would make it real. "Stop!" Her voice came out whiny and thin.

They were in the first layer of trees. Leah reached her free hand to grab a branch. He tugged and the skin on her palm ripped open. She cried out, and then there was a whirl of movement. Something made a clanging sound like a gong, and Leah felt the ironlike grip on her arm loosen and fall away. She fell backward and there was Sam, moving in slow motion, a shovel raised like a baseball bat. The shovel bit into the man's side and he dropped to his knees. Another yawning arc of shovel and *clang*. The man was curled up on the ground, not moving. The moment gathered like a drop at the tip of a faucet, then suddenly time resumed.

Leah scuttled backward like a crab and stood up. Sam kicked the man savagely in the side. The man groaned.

Sam dropped the shovel and turned to Leah, a horrible, savage look in his eyes.

"The truck," he rasped.

In a flash they were back at the road. Leah tossed her pack into the back and heard it land with a clatter in a pile of tools. She ran around to the driver's side and yanked open the door. "Keys, keys, keys," she begged. They were on the seat. Her hand was shaking so badly that she had to stab at the ignition four times before the key slid in. Sam landed heavily on the seat next to her and locked the door.

"Drive," he gasped.

The engine sputtered to life and Leah yanked the gearshift into drive. There was a squeal of rubber and rasp of gravel, then they lurched forward onto the road.

Leah was breathing so quickly that she thought she might start to hyperventilate. Without realizing it, she accelerated to seventy-five miles per hour.

Up ahead three abandoned cars were blocking the shoulder. Sam braced his hands against the dashboard, expecting to crash, but they squirted through the narrow gap like a watermelon seed.

Sam removed his hands from the dash and folded in on himself.

"Sorry," said Leah. She took her foot off the accelerator and then braked suddenly. Swerving to the side of the road, Leah wrenched the truck to a stop, threw open the door and vomited onto the running board. She hunched, gasping for a count of five breaths and then sat up and wiped her mouth with the back of her trembling hand.

"Jesus," she said.

This time she pulled out slowly. She looked at Sam.

His face was all squeezed up and red. Tears glinted in the crevices his expression created and a bubble of snot was growing over his top lip.

"Did he hurt you? Sam, are you okay?" Leah swerved with alarm.

"I shoulda killed him," croaked Sam. "I should have gotten a gun and I should have killed him." His voice cracked and he swiped furiously at his nose with the back of his hand.

Leah knew somehow that he was not talking about the man they'd just left. "Who?" Then the answer came to her. "Your dad?"

"He's not my real dad!" Sam shouted at her. "I'm adopted!" His shoulders began to shake.

"He did *that* to *you*?" Leah was crying now too.

Sam rolled down his window and a deafening cyclone filled the truck.

The words "rape" and "abuse" soured Leah's tongue. She realized that saying them aloud at this moment would be both cruel and unnecessary.

She let her hand slide across the seat and fumble for Sam's.

"Hey!" she shouted over the wind. "You saved me again! Three times now!" She squeezed and felt a weak squeeze back. "You know what that means?"

Sam turned his head toward her. He looked tired, like he was a million years old. "What?"

"We're family now, okay?"

They were about forty miles from home. The gas tank was nearly empty, but they would drive the truck until it died and then leave it on the side of the road for that terrible man to find or not.

And *nobody*, thought Leah, *nobody* will hurt Sam again.

# Chapter Thirty-One: Brownie Mix

### Margot

I wrote letters to Leah in my head. They started off as texts and then e-mails, but then even my imagination went analog. They were letters that described how Ronan's skin was half a degree warmer than mine, even his fingers. I told her about my suspicion that Mom had a sixth sense for quashing romance, since she'd found a way to interrupt us three times just when things were getting interesting. I told her the news that the government sent out census takers and was promising food, possibly within a week. I told her to hurry up and come home because I thought she should invent a pedal-powered washing machine, and I wanted her to meet my chickens. I told her about shooting the dog, how Dad and Ronan buried it before I came back up from the smoker and how Grandma actually suggested eating it, but Mom gave her such a look that she never mentioned it again.

So that's what I was doing in my head. With my body I was looking for chicken eggs, since the ladies were really sneaky about where they laid. I had wriggled behind the forsythia in the yard and was trying to look for eggs without getting an eye poked out when I heard that *A-WOOO-GA!* honking sound of an old-fashioned car horn. It got closer. *A-WOO-GA! A-WOO-GA!*

and then a really old Volkswagen Bug that might have been orange at some point turned down our driveway and shuddered to a halt.

I saw a kid leaning into the front seat, pushing the horn over and over, and after a second I realized it was my cousin Caleb, and that the smiling man in the driver's seat was Uncle Jerry. Then one of the back doors pushed open and there she was.

My sister.

We all started running. I heard a cry that you would usually associate with natives in war paint, a cry so foreign I couldn't identify it as happy or sad, but then I saw Mom sprinting in from the pasture, actually sprinting and howling at the same time. And then I was hugging Leah and smelling her smell and I felt the thud of Mom hitting us and then Lucas and then Dad and then we were all wailing. Even Lucas was sobbing openly.

We stood in the warm, stinking huddle doing little hops for at least a minute before I noticed that Caleb and Uncle Jerry and Aunt Alice were in their own huddle with Grandma, and that there was one more person who was not in a huddle. Leah noticed too and she snaked her arm out of the mass of our family and tugged the person into our human tepee. He was a boy with fair coloring and big ears. He was turning bright red before our eyes.

"Guys," said Leah, smiling, "this is Sam. He saved my life and he's going to be a part of our family now."

It took a few seconds for us to digest that and then we hugged Sam and then Leah and then each other, and then I began to wish that we had done all this hugging back when personal hygiene was a higher priority.

It turned out that Leah and Sam walked practically all the way here from Maine and then got picked up on the side of the road by Uncle Jerry just five miles down the road. Caleb and Uncle Jerry had fought off pirates in the middle of Lake Michigan and then driven here in a car that might just fall apart in the driveway. There was something about a motorcycle and a storm, and Leah mentioned huts crews, and I told them about everything here, and it took all afternoon just to get everybody's stories straight. Nobody worked for the rest of the day. We just sat and listened to one another and watched my chickens roaming the yard. We all kept touching one another's wrists or hair, like we couldn't get over the miracle of being there.

We celebrated by turning on the generator so that we could bake some brownies from a box of mix. We ate food from Leah's pack and from Uncle Jerry, and just the fact that it was different from what we'd been eating made it taste amazing.

That night Lucas slept in Mom and Dad's room, Grandma and Uncle Jerry slept in Lucas's room, and Aunt Alice and Caleb slept in Leah's room. I hoped that Caleb liked sleeping near his mom, because I didn't think she was going to let him out of her sight for a very long time.

Sam and Leah rolled out their sleeping bags on the floor in my room, but after an hour of listening to all the extra breathing I couldn't sleep.

"Leah?" I whispered.

"Yeah."

"You awake?"

Leah chuckled.

"Come up here," I whispered.

I heard rustling and then the bed dipped and Leah climbed in next to me.

"Hey," she whispered.

"Is Sam your boyfriend?"

"No. It's not like that."

"So did he really save your life?"

"Yeah."

Leah told me all of it, and when she got to the part about the seat belt burn, we cried. When she told me that Sam actually was the senator's son, I hooted and she shushed me.

"Don't tell anyone, okay?"

Then finally I got to tell Leah about Ronan, and even though I'd been imagining how I'd tell her every single little detail, when it came right down to it, I just said I really liked him and that he was actually a tiny bit nerdy when it came to gardening.

"Hey, Margot," whispered Leah as we were drifting off to sleep.

"What?"

"Nice boobs."

I poked Leah in the side and went to sleep even though the bed was jiggling with Leah's laughter.

# Epilogue: Three Months Later

## Margot

One in ten Americans died during the Blackout, though here in Vermont that number was smaller because of our sparse population and open land. Even so, almost everybody we know lost family to the dysentery that swept over Boston, the cholera in New York, the unrelenting heat in the South, the famine that hit almost everywhere. Some people are still trying to find family members or friends. Judy came back exactly one month after she left, but she still hasn't heard from her cousin in New York or the rest of her mom's family.

Our family has been lucky, though, and not just because nobody died. The interim government designated us a dairy and chicken farm because of our pasture, fence, and water. Two months ago sixteen Holstein dairy cows and one hundred chickens showed up from Iowa. The government is trying to redistribute food sources so that it doesn't take so much gas and energy to feed Americans. Now everyday people from our area take their coupons and come on their bikes to get milk and eggs from us. Few people have refrigeration yet, since power is on only two hours a day, but since folks easily eat up their rations every day, they don't go bad. Eggs, if you don't wash them, will stay good for weeks. The next step is to figure out cheese, which would be a good way to store extra milk.

On weekdays Lucas, Judy, Dad, and I ride our bikes the mile and a half to the main road and a bus comes and takes us to school. There is gas now for "high-priority vehicles" but almost nothing else. Everybody has a bike, even old people, and we take up the whole road when we ride places together.

At school, paper is pretty much sacred, so we use it only for homework assignments, and everybody has learned to write small. You can tell that teachers are really happy that we finally have to learn how to spell things, since there is no spell-check anymore. The best part about school is lunch, since the school food is provided by the state. You better believe that we all eat every last crumb.

There are no sports after school anymore, but they've put kids to work replanting trees, since folks chopped down so many to make fires. One and a half hours will earn you an extra point on your ration card. You can join a work crew, salvaging abandoned buildings, or help redistribute the stuff we pulled in off the highways. Some people have city refugees in their homes. Everybody wants a woodstove and a solar panel. At school a group of kids figured out how to make electricity by pedaling stationary bikes. They hooked the bikes up to old computers and took turns playing Tetris. When the teachers found out, they attached the bikes to radios, so now every morning we all hear the news accompanied by the sound of furious pedaling.

The news is this: General Amandon is acting president until we can set up an election. He tells us that the blackouts are an opportunity to purge the government. He says that the computer virus was released by a faction of his party who wanted to wipe out every last trace of wealth—no stocks or bonds, no savings accounts, no patents or copyrights. That faction was the more extreme end of General Amandon's party, which is called We the People. WTP believed that something had to be done about the ways that the government perpetuated income inequality, so they did it. No one person is actually claiming responsibility for anything, so Dad thinks Amandon did it. It feels a little weird that we get all our national news from the government because no one else has recovered from the Blackout yet. Amandon promises a fair election and a repeal of *Citizens United.*

It is as if the Blackout added ten years to all our ages. We are not treated as kids anymore. Nobody supervises everything we do. We talk about politics all the time. It's not like it was before, when everybody had their own news source and nobody could tell what was true or not. We all hear the same news every morning, and so now we discuss what we think about it, not if what we heard was true or not. We ask one another, should the government give farmers gas rations or should the farmers charge more money for food? How do we heat our houses this winter? Should the government distribute fuel to save the forests? Should it be based on family size or house size? How do you distribute two hours' worth of electricity so that it is fair? We are learning to disagree with one another in an agreeable way. We're learning to debate without making it personal.

Caleb, Uncle Jerry, and Aunt Alice left for Nantucket a while back, and so far we've only gotten this letter:

*Dear Family,*
*We are well. We delivered Doc's effects to his house*
*on Nantucket, but finding it empty, we have decided*
*to stay here. I am very busy importing and installing*
*solar panels. I have a new boat, Doc's Scalpel.*
*She's a 30-foot sailboat and can make it to the*

*mainland in under two hours with a good wind. This old dog is learning a few new tricks.*

*We hope you are well. Karen, I am sending along this purse that Alice says you'll love. Alan, how's that cold storage coming? Tell Leah and Margot and Lucas I could use somebody with half a brain to help me with all this electrical stuff.*

*—Jer*


*P.S. The Volkswagen made it all the way to Rhode Island but died before we could figure out how to get her across to the island. I found an old Porsche. I am working on that. Dad says it will pay for college if I can get it going. Mom says it may be a while before people are buying vintage luxury vehicles. I go to school in a restaurant with only 49 other kids. I am the tallest in my class. Finally. I am sick of eating fish but am getting really good at fishing. We are saving up for a motorcycle. —Caleb*


Grandma read the letter and was very grumpy. "Where did they get a boat? Does this mean that they are married again? Isn't it just like Jerry to send a letter that only tells you enough to have a hundred more questions?"

Mom was funny about the purse.

"It's a Birkin," she sighed, and then sniffed the inside. She brings it out to the barn with her and uses it to collect ration tickets. Every once in a while I see her loop it over her elbow and strut down the path to the pasture.

218

During the week Leah lives in Montpelier, where she is part of an emergency task force to see what can be done about salvaging the tech that got melted from the virus. Every Wednesday we talk to her on the landline that they've fixed in the library. She sounds happy and comes home on the weekend with hard-to-get things like fruit and coffee.

It turns out that Sam is our "cow whisperer." He told us all that he's eighteen, which doesn't seem likely, but if he doesn't want to go to school and would rather stay home worrying about hay, that's fine with us. None of us really wanted to run a dairy, but it was either that or move out so that somebody else could run it. We would have figured it out, I guess, but Sam actually loves it. He's good friends with the old man from the post office, because he used to have a dairy. Sam takes care of the animals, Mom distributes the rations, and Grandma is figuring out how to finish the new barn before winter sets in.

Ronan practically lived with us during the vegetable harvest and that was just fine by me. I'm grateful that I have boobies to distract him with when he starts talking about crop rotation or staggering harvest times. He'll get his medicine, too, and it's not nearly as expensive as it used to be. The government helped pharmaceutical companies get restarted, but in return, for one year, the pharma companies are allowed to charge only what it costs to make the drugs and they're allowed to make only drugs that are on the priority list. Ronan's medicine made the list. Grandma's cholesterol pills did not. She read somewhere that free-range chicken and beef have a lot less bad cholesterol, so she says she's not worried.

So what next?

We chop wood. We insulate our houses as best we can and close off extra rooms. We set traps for critters that like to eat chickens as much as we do. We soak udders and read up on cheese. We bike. We fix things and learn to sew. In November we'll elect a president, and I'd bet you a bar of chocolate that voter turnout will be the highest it's ever been. We mourn our dead and miss our friends who are no longer a telephone call away.

The big difference is that we are grateful. It gets dark early these days, so my mom lights a lantern in the living room and we all sit around the one light and read or do homework or sketch or plan. We wear slippers and sweaters and Grandma and I usually share a blanket on the couch, but it is not terribly cold yet. I look around the bowl of light in that dark room and each of my family's faces is lit up, warm and yellow. We have what we need. We have a task for each day. We have each other.

# Hope A. C. Bentley

I had the kind of childhood that generally does not create great art since it was almost cartoonishly happy. My brothers and I had doting parents, wonderful friends and the run of an idyllic little village in Connecticut.

Most of my writing is a sort of wish fulfillment; what if there really was magic in the world? What if we had to go back to the pioneer days? What if we could bring back the souls of people we love?

I started Golden Light Factory because I love igniting curiosity in young people, and I believe that books have the power to do that.

I live with my hubby, three children and several chickens in an idyllic little village in Vermont.